FINDING OUT

JENNI BARA

Finding Out

Boston Revs Three Outs Book 4

Line Copy and Proof Editing by VB Edits

Final Proofreading by Jeffrey Hodge

Interior formatting Sara Stewart

Cover by Cheslea Kemp

ISBN: 978-1-959389-17-0 (ebook)

ISBN: 978-1-959389-26-2 (paperback)

ISBN: 978-1-959389-27-9 (hardback)

Jennibara.com

Finding Out

BOSTON REVS THREE OUTS BOOK 4

Jenni Bara

DEDICATION

The all for Boston Revs fans who told me they needed this book...you're welcome.

Playlist

All For You - Sister Hazel

Dust on the Bottle - David Lee Murphy

Come Over - Kenny Chesney

Lavender Haze - Taylor Swift

Chemical - Post Malone

I Won't Back Down - Tom Petty

(You Drive Me) Crazy - Britney Spears

I Like Me Better - Lauv

Style - Taylor Swift

Nothin' Like You - Dan + Shay

One Man Band - Old Dominion

The Good Ones - Gabby Barrett

Remember That Night? - Sara Kays

Can't Stop This Thing We Started -
Bryan Adams

Cinderella - Steven Curtis Chapman

I Don't Dance - Lee Brice

BOSTON REVS BASEBALL CLUB

Can't wait to see you all at Spring Training!

LINEUP

COACH: TOM WILSON #49

1 KYLE BOSCO #29   RF

2 JASPER QUINN #16   1B

3 EMERSON KNIGHT #21   3B

4 ASHER PRICE #5   C

5 HENRY WINTERS #44   2B

6 EDDIE MARTINEZ #30   SS

7 COLTON STEWART #23   DH

8 TRISTIAN JENNER #27   LF

9 MASON DUMPTY #22   CF

P CHRISTIAN DAMIANO #35   P

B

Wren

1

"GUESS who gets to see New York at Christmas?" Dressed in a suit, as always, my boss, Pat, leaned his shoulder against the doorframe.

With my elbows on my small desk, I tucked my hands under my chin and put on my best pout. "You're just being mean at this point."

I'd begged him to send me to New York this weekend. But after six years, Pat had become immune to my puppy-dog eyes, and the *no* had flown from his lips easily.

Seeing the city that never sleeps at Christmas wasn't my priority, honestly. I'd seen the Macy's lights, the windows at Saks, and Rocke-feller center plenty of times in my life. I'd even had the privilege of watching the Rockettes on stage a few times growing up. The magic of a New York Christmas wasn't the draw.

No, I was desperate to tag along to the private sale of one of the most famous pieces the Boston Auction House had sold since I'd been hired. I'd been told that I could come across as shallow, and maybe that was true, but not when it came to art.

"Mean, really? Even if the person I'm talking about is *you*?" The corner of Pat's lips lifted at the end of the sentence.

I bolted upright in my chair, my heart hammering.

No way.

"What?" I clasped my hands in my lap, afraid to hope.

Please don't let him be messing with me.

My love for visual art ran deep. The message a painting could convey was like nothing else.

Stonehenge, by John Constable, was a masterpiece. I'd hardly had the opportunity to enjoy it last year when we priced it out for the owners. So not only was I yearning to experience a transfer of a piece of this caliber, but I wanted to spend a little more time in its presence. Soak in each brushstroke. Wonder how the artist had brought the clouds to life. Study the subtle details that allowed the blend of colors to make each rock pop against the almost gray sky. I wanted to sit in the deep feelings the painting pulled from my soul.

When a piece of art spoke so loudly it echoed through my body like this one had, it was impossible not to long to see it again.

"Larry's youngest is in the hospital."

I sucked in a breath, and my heart crashed into my stomach. I wanted this opportunity, but not because of someone else's misfortune. Larry was a nice guy. He lived one of those perfect lives, with a home on Long Island, a white picket fence, and three cute-as-hell kids.

"Oh no." I swallowed the lump in my throat. "Is he okay?"

"It's a combination of pneumonia and asthma." Pat frowned from the doorway.

I couldn't blame him for hovering there. My office was the size of a closet. There was hardly enough room for my desk and one extra chair.

"Larry says it's precautionary, but even so, he can't leave."

"Of course." Larry was the kind of guy who took off for T-ball practice. There was no way he'd leave his wife or his son during an emergency. "So…" I nibbled on my bottom lip. God, I was an awful person for it, but now that I knew Larry's emergency wasn't dire, excitement was pounding through me. "I get to go?"

"Not only are you going, but you're it."

My heart skipped as I gaped at him. This moment was surreal. Until now, I'd thought I had no chance. The customer we'd arranged the purchase for had literally refused to allow me to be involved with his account at all. He wouldn't even speak to me if Larry wasn't available. "I get to run point?"

Pat nodded. "Diana has tickets to Pops Holiday at Symphony Hall this weekend." Tight lines formed around his eyes. His wife was a former cellist and a loyal patron of Boston's Symphony. If he skipped one of their biggest performances of the year, I could only imagine Diana's wrath. "Since I have no interest in getting a divorce for Christmas, I can't travel." He clapped his hands and rubbed them together. "But." He gave me a pointed look. "That doesn't mean I expect this transfer to go anything but perfectly."

"Of course." Excitement bubbled up my chest, but I forced myself not to beam too brightly. Professionalism, that was my goal.

"Good. As you know, this client is…" He rocked back on his heels. "Picky."

Difficult. Demanding. Frustrating. According to Larry, at least. I wouldn't know because I'd never even spoken to the guy. It was as if his identity was a national secret or something. To a certain extent, I could understand, I supposed. The buyer was paying millions for this piece, and it wouldn't be wise to advertise that. Art theft was real and rampant. Discretion was important in our business, but we rarely kept secrets from those who worked within these walls.

"I can handle anyone," I promised, confidence settling me.

I excelled at schmoozing. I'd practically been born to do it, and I'd absolutely been trained to be social. My whole life, my parents had dreamed I'd become the wife of a senator or a businessman who consistently sat on the *Forbes* Top 100 list. Clearly I'd missed the mark. I was no one's wife. Not that they ever let the idea of me getting married go.

Pat gave a clipped nod. "I don't doubt your social skills, but *everyone's* watching this one."

I cocked a brow.

"Cliff is leaving after Christmas. It hasn't been formally announced yet, but I'll move into his role at the first of the year."

I forced myself not to react to the way he was studying me. I'd been hearing this rumor for a couple of weeks, and damn, I wanted his job. I'd been slowly working my way up for the last six years. I wasn't the only woman here, not by a longshot, but most of the females in employment were in acquisitions, and very few made it to management. Long hours and late nights made it difficult to find an acceptable work-life balance. For me, that wasn't an issue. I didn't have kids, heck, I didn't even do relationships. I just had a drive to move up, and Pat's job came with a nice title, a pay raise, and several staff members under him.

"Erin would love to have more females in management roles." He shrugged, nonchalant, as he dropped that crumb of information.

"You know I'm gunning for her job someday." I smirked. I'd interned under the head of our auction house the summer after I got my master's degree from NYU. The woman was a force. A total badass. She was exactly what I wanted to be. When I'd finished my three months with her, Erin had offered me a job. It was entry level— literally checking in the paintings and setting up the displays for the weekly auctions—but I jumped at the opportunity. And six years later, I'd been promoted several times and the two of us still met for monthly dinners.

"Even Erin knows that." Larry chuckled. "I'll email you the flight info and everything you need."

"Perfect." Satisfaction swelled in my chest. This whole thing had made my day. Hell, it'd made my month.

Pat lifted his chin and gave me a small smile. "Get out of here. It's almost eight; everyone else left hours ago."

They had, but this was my thing. I thrived on working long hours, learning the details of each piece for the next auction, and searching out up-and-coming artists. I was running the auction on Sunday night, so I was here ensuring that every detail would be perfect. Putting in the extra effort like this was what made me stand out. It was how I knew I was on the short list for Pat's job.

"Go home." He tipped his head toward the elevator down the hall.

I gave him a mock salute. "Yes, sir."

With a chuckle, he left me alone in my office.

I sat back in my chair, staring at the watercolor hanging opposite my desk, yet not actually seeing it. This was my break. The opportunity I needed to move out of the windowless room and down the hall to management. Finally.

I pulled out my phone.

> Me: GUESS WHAT?

> Avery: You didn't listen to me and went ahead and bought yourself the bondage-like Louie shoes for the WAGs party next week.

Ha. Of course I had. Though I can't imagine either of my best friends would be surprised by that. And that kind of news? It did not warrant a message in all caps. I wasn't a wife or girlfriend of any of the Boston Revs baseball players, but since Avery was both the coach's daughter and the star pitcher's fiancée, my bestie always made sure I got to tag along to the fun professional baseball events.

> Jana: You finally broke the dry spell and gave in to the hot intern.

I rolled my eyes. Even if it had been months, I had zero intention of messing around at work. I had goals, and I wouldn't risk compromising them. A fling wasn't worth the risk, and men tended to find me intimidating. I said what I thought and knew what I needed, and I didn't put up with crap. Somehow that made men wither around me.

> Me: Seriously? Those are your guesses for my all-caps message?

> Jana: What would you guess if I'd said that?

> Me: A bird shit on Chris again, and this time you got it on video.

> Jana worked with Avery at the Boston Zoo, and their stories made me cackle. Especially when they included Avery's very grumpy, very germophobic fiancé.

> Jana: GIF of a girl spitting out her coffee

> Jana: Yeah, that would be worth an all-caps message.

> Avery: Don't pick on my fiancé.

> Me: We love Chris.

It was the truth, even if his issues with germs and cleanliness meshed poorly with our girl's job as the head of avian medicine at the Boston Zoo.

> Jana: Of course we love your man. We even let him tag along to girls' night.

> Avery: Let him? Ha. You two make him come.

> Avery: GIF of an eye roll

> Avery: Anyway…what's the big news?

> Me: I'm going to New York! I got lead on the secret project.

> Avery: GIF of fireworks

> Jana: That's AWESOME.

> Avery: Congrats!!!!

> Me: Yeah, so no girls' night out this weekend.

> Avery: Chris will be crushed.

> Jana: Dead. Skull emoji, skull emoji

Chuckling, I dropped my phone into my bag. Chris might be the best thing that ever happened to my bestie, but fun was not his middle name. I couldn't complain. He loved our girl enough to put up with Jana and me without a single complaint. The man lived by the mantra that if Avery loved it, then he did too. #boyfriendgoals. Or I guess #husbandgoals would be more appropriate.

As I set my phone down, I smiled at the framed photo of Jana, Avery, and me that I kept on my desk. We'd been the three musketeers for years now, but Avery's wedding was next month, and Jana had finally given the guy she'd been dating the boyfriend label, so things had changed a lot lately. I couldn't say I was sad about it. I had my career, and one day, I'd be kick-ass Auntie Wren to the slew of kids my friends produced.

I unplugged my laptop and dropped it into my bag, then tucked my Stanley bottle and my glasses inside.

Two minutes later, I was stepping onto the elevator to head out but was stopped when a voice called out.

"Hold it."

I threw an arm out and caught the door just before it closed completely, and as it bounced back open, a black heel appeared against the silver floor and Erin stepped on.

"Wren." Smiling, she tucked a strand of long blond hair behind her ear. She was the epitome of professional in her stylish suits and expensive heels. "I hear you have a big weekend."

Giddiness coursed through me, but I schooled my expression and nodded. "Thanks for giving me the chance."

"Thank Pat," she said. She always made it clear that although she loved seeing me succeed and was happy to give me advice along the way, my achievements were my own. "A word of advice, though."

I tipped my head, eager, like I always was, for any tidbit of information she had for me.

"In our business, it's important for everyone, but especially women, to remain professional, regardless of the situation or who the client might be." She pursed her lips.

"Of course." I let out a breath of relief. I prided myself on my ability to be professional no matter what.

She cocked a brow. "Just keep that in mind this weekend."

I nodded and gave her a grateful smile, but in the back of my mind, I couldn't help but wonder who exactly I'd be dealing with.

Daddy Wilson

2

ONE OF THE many things I appreciated about Larry was that he never showed up late. So as I sat alone in first class, I couldn't help but be concerned. This weekend was the culmination of years of planning. Owning *Stonehenge* had been a dream of mine since before I was thirty. Back when I'd first seen it and didn't have anywhere near the capital to buy it. Twenty years later, the anxiety of being so close to calling the painting mine had my stress level at an all-time high. And now the man who'd been working with me to broker this deal was MIA.

I'd texted him just before boarding the flight to New York and again after I'd been seated, but he'd yet to respond. Yesterday I had gotten a vague email that mentioned a small change of plans that was accompanied by a comment about how I shouldn't worry, that everything would go off without a hitch.

Yet here I was, stewing in anxiety.

This was all totally out of character for the man I'd been working with for almost a year.

Locking my jaw, I did something I hated to do. I went over his head.

> Me: What's going on? I'm on the plane, but I've
> yet to see or even hear from Larry.

The bubbles appeared instantly, sending a strange mixture of relief and apprehension through me.

> Pat: Larry's son is in the hospital.

My stomached dropped. Damn. I wasn't an asshole. I wouldn't throw a fit about Larry's absence. I couldn't imagine the fear of having a child in the hospital. My little girl, who, at twenty-eight, wasn't little anymore, had been my world.

My chest twisted at the thought of her. Avery was getting married next month. Her fiancé, although not what I would have picked for her if I'd had the privilege, was a good man. She'd fallen in love with one of my baseball players, which wasn't ideal. I'd been with the Boston Revs for years, first as a pitcher and eventually working my way up the coaching chain, until ten years ago, when I was named head coach. And the biggest pain in my ass in the whole franchise? Naturally, it was my soon-to-be son-in-law.

I roughed a hand down my face and sighed. I couldn't even be mad about it, because Christian Damiano worshipped the ground my daughter walked on.

Our lives were changing, because for years it was baseball and being Avery's dad. That's all I was. Now I had to figure out what else there was out there for me because she was moving on.

When my phone buzzed in my hand, I shook away the thoughts.

> Pat: Don't worry. We have our best headed
> your way. You'll love her.

I winced at the *her*. It wasn't that I didn't believe a woman could do this job as well as a man. The issue was that this meant I'd be spending the night in New York with a woman. And not just in New York, but in the same two-bedroom suite. Larry and I had arranged it this way in order to keep two sets of eyes on the art. We'd planned to order room service, and from there, I was sure he'd pick my brain about the upcoming baseball season. The guy loved the Revs, and I was happy to entertain him for a few hours.

This, though, changed things. Who was the woman Pat had mentioned? If Erin Stanbright, the head of the auction house, were the one accompanying me, she would have texted me herself. She and I went way back. But any other woman had the potential to be chaos, and I liked order.

"I would love that."

At the sound of that sultry voice, my entire being lit up.

On instinct, I turned to my left, following the sound. But when I locked on its source, I froze.

No.

My every muscle tensed, and it took conscious effort to fight the sensation that swamped me. The same sensation I'd warred with for years.

I pulled a hard breath in through my nose and took her in from beneath the brim of my cap.

She wore a tight white sweater and high-waisted black pants. The look was rounded out with silky dark hair and plush, pouty lips.

My living, breathing nightmare had appeared in front of me, just as sexy as ever as she smiled at the man who'd probably tripped over himself to help her hoist her bag into the overhead compartment. For a few beats, I got to watch her, unnoticed, as she thanked her good Samaritan.

As the man stumbled to his own seat, she turned my way, a smile at the ready. "Hi, Mr. Brown. I'm thrill…" The words trailed off, and her smile melted away as recognition flooded her deep onyx eyes. She cleared her throat, hardly missing a beat, and continued. "Thrilled to assist you this weekend. I guarantee this adventure will be painless for you."

Holding my breath, I pressed my phone into the armrest. Painless? Nothing about being in the proximity of Wren Jacobs would be painless. The woman might be my daughter's best friend, but I had no doubt that she had been put on this earth to torture me.

"Sit," I gritted out.

In a very un-Wren-like move, she listened. Silently, she dropped into the seat next to me. The move sent her expensive scent wafting over me, filling my nose and haunting me as it had every time I'd seen her for the last few years.

"Mr. Brown—"

"Wren." I cut her off. We weren't doing this. I would not spend the next twenty-four hours with someone I'd known for more than fifteen years pretending my name was Mr. Brown. "Cut the crap."

She cocked her perfectly sculpted brow and leaned so close, the heat of her body radiated through me, causing my heart to pound in my ears. "Would you prefer Daddy Wilson?"

Those words rocked through me like an electric jolt. Just like they did every time they left her lips. I hated myself for the inappropriate reaction. I'd known Wren since well before she was old enough to be thought of in the way I was right this second. She had grown up with my daughter, and when Avery left for college on the West Coast, nineteen-year-old Wren left my life as well. During the six-year gap, I'd been busy with baseball, and when she returned as a twenty-five-year-old woman, breezing into my kitchen with my daughter, she was unrecognizable. Sleek, confident, gorgeous. And when the *Daddy Wilson* slipped from her lips like it had a million times before, my body had buzzed in a way that was absolutely inappropriate in response to a woman nineteen years my junior.

"Mr. Wilson," I corrected through gritted teeth. Although, fucking hell, that was only slightly better. "Better yet, this weekend, I'm Tom."

"Okay."

Jesus, if I'd known she'd respond so reasonably to my first name, I'd have suggested it years ago. "Good."

She shrugged, the move shifting her closer once more. "I should be shocked, but this makes so much sense. Our conversation about *Stonehenge* last spring should have been the only clue I needed."

In vivid detail, my brain ran over that night. Wren seated across from me at O'Hannigan's, her hand tucked under her chin as she talked about the swirl of each brushstroke that created the haze of gray clouds. God, I'd been hypnotized by her passion about my favorite work of art. So much so that I'd totally missed the way my colleague was flirting with my daughter two seats away.

Wren cleared her throat, pulling me back to the present. She lifted her chin a fraction, making it difficult not to focus on the smooth skin of her neck. "For the record, I understand that it's probably hard for you to trust the kid who was always getting your daughter into trouble to be lead on this project."

Eyes narrowed, I assessed her. Sure, Wren had been a hellion as a teenager and probably still was, but that wasn't the issue. Erin had been very clear when we started this project that Wren was the best. The up-and-coming star who would someday be her right-hand woman. But I'd told her that I preferred not to work with her because of her personal connection to Avery. The truth of it, though, was that I didn't trust myself to spend too much time with my daughter's best friend. Not only would Avery be appalled if she knew the kinds of thoughts that ran through my mind, but Heath Jacobs, a longtime friend, would surely kill me if he knew that I'd been fantasizing about his daughter. If I made even a single move, I'd be buried under the tee box of the first hole at his country club before I could utter an apology.

"This weekend, I'm going to prove that you should have been working with me all this time." She shifted away with a huff.

Part of me wanted to close the gap she'd created, but over the years, I'd perfected the art of keeping my distance. I couldn't leave the issue of her talent hanging, though. I'd hate myself if I made her doubt abilities even a little.

"I know you're more than capable of managing this transfer," I muttered. "We all know you'll handle it even better than Larry would have."

Lips parting, she studied me, an unnamed emotion swimming in her eyes. A feeling I thought might match the flutter in my chest.

"Can I get you a preflight beverage?"

Wren took a breath and blinked, and instantly, the emotion was gone.

"Coffee, extra milk, and two sugars, please." She gave the flight attendant a polite smile. "Mr. Brown needs a black coffee. In a ceramic mug. He won't drink out of paper."

It annoyed me that she knew me well enough to order correctly, while at the same time, the idea settled warmly in my bones, relaxing me. This was a good indication that she might have this weekend locked down.

She watched the flight attendant scurry back to the galley before she shifted those onyx eyes back my way.

"I have work to do, but if you need something, don't hesitate to ask." Without waiting for a response, she pulled her iPad out of her bag and popped in her earbuds.

I tried to ignore the woman next to me, but ten minutes into the flight, I found myself trying to eye her tablet.

An image of my painting—or the work of art that would soon be mine—was on her screen, and she'd zoomed in on a small rip at the edge of the canvas.

"Is that bigger than a half inch?" I demanded. I was aware that there was a small imperfection caused by reframing, but in the photo, it looked bigger than the seller had claimed.

She popped one ear bud out. "I hope not, but don't worry, I'll check." She shifted the screen toward me and leaned closer.

Her arm brushed my chest, causing my abs to tense. I could not react this way. She was my daughter's best friend. Nineteen fucking years younger than me. And yet here I was, a creepy old asshole drooling over her.

"See here?" She pointed to the top right corner of the screen.

Once again I was flooded with that sweet perfume, the scent making my heart race. It took far too much effort to maintain my self-control.

Wren Jacobs would not be the woman who broke me.

"That's the scale."

I blinked, attempting to think about anything other than the warmth of her arm pressing against mine. The way her chest lifted with each intake of air. The way I longed to close the space between us.

"According to this…"

I had lost the entire conversation.

"Not even three-eighths of an inch."

She reached over and patted my thigh, the warmth of her palm ripping through me.

"It's rare when bigger isn't better, huh?" She laughed, the sound causing my dick to twitch.

Clearing my throat, I straightened. "The only people who say that buy cars to overcompensate for what they're lacking."

Wren chuckled. "Whereas you buy paintings to...?"

"To set a mood."

My arm brushed hers on the armrest between us, and instantly, goose bumps broke out on her skin. I wasn't blind to her reaction to me. This attraction wasn't one-sided, not by a longshot. And that only made my vow to not act on it more difficult. "Art creates emotions and sets a tone."

Her pulse fluttered in her neck as she regarded me. Fuck, how I'd love to press my tongue against it and feel each beat.

"A tone for what?" The breathy whisper floated around us, making it impossible not to glance down to her mouth. When her tongue snaked out to wet her bottom lip, my body reacted like it had run along my skin.

Damn. I looked away.

"For whatever I want." I turned toward the window. Shit. I couldn't keep engaging her. Not if I wanted to distance myself.

Once I'd averted my attention, she made no attempt to start a conversation again. Besides ordering a second cup of coffee for each of us—decaf for me, because clearly, she knew I only had two cups of regular a day—she was silent. Focused. It was strange, sitting beside her. I almost felt at ease. That was until the plane had taxied to the gate and the young asswipe in the suit across the row attempted to get her bag.

"I've got it." The words were almost a snarl.

His eyes widened, and with his hands held up in front of him, he stepped away.

As I pulled her bag down and settled it on my shoulder, Wren cocked that thin brow at me. I ignored the look. What was so wrong with carrying her bag like any decent man would?

"Go." I waved a hand toward the front of the plane.

She smirked. "If I wasn't on my best professional behavior, I'd have to say that growl was hot AF, Daddy Wilson."

My gut tightened, and my entire body buzzed with anticipation. Fuck. By now, my damn dick should have realized that I wasn't going there. But the response was ingrained in me. As she spun, I couldn't help but zero in on the perfect curve of her ass in those black pants. A groan worked its way up my throat, but I bit it back before it could escape. This was going to be a long two days.

Wren
3

"THANKS." I smiled at the young guy behind the hotel desk.

"Text us if you need anything at all, Ms. Jacobs. Our virtual concierge service is top tier." As he passed me the keys to the suite the auction house had reserved, his gaze slipped over my head to the hulk of a man glaring at pretty much everyone.

It didn't matter that Tom Wilson was in jeans and had a baseball cap pulled low to obscure his face. The man couldn't do low-profile. I didn't know whether the concierge recognized him as the famous former baseball god he was or the coach of the Boston Revs, but it didn't matter. Tom's presence was bigger than his reputation.

And the tight T-shirt didn't help.

My stomach flipped as I took in the muscles barely hidden by gray fabric. It was unfair, a man of his age with shoulders and pecs of stone. Not an inch of his body had aged in all the years I'd known him. It was difficult to believe he was in his late forties. Hardly a wrinkle pulled at the skin around his bright blue eyes, and the light brown hair that peeked out from beneath his Boston Bolts cap was barely flecked with gray. I swore the man had single-handedly learned the secret of how not to age. The rest of the world changed, grew older, yet he stayed forever young.

But I'd been crushing on Tom Wilson since the time I'd understood what it was to have a crush. At one of the Rev's player's wife's birthday party last month, I'd enjoyed the hell out of wiggling my way past his steel will to get a reaction out of the rigid man. And I swore, that night at Zara's party, was one of those times he saw me for the woman I was and not the girl I used to be.

Excitement tingled through my stomach. There had been times over the last two years that I could have sworn Daddy Wilson was looking at me. When I thought that maybe the growls he fired my way weren't brought on by annoyance but attraction. I'd never been certain until this moment.

"Are you not freezing?"

With the way he was looking at me, I felt anything but cold.

His attention heated me through, and not only did it have my lips lifting into a smile, but it made my confidence soar.

"Don't you know the expression beauty knows no pain, Daddy Wilson?"

His frown deepened, but as his eyes lifted to mine, the spark of interest still burned bright.

"Mr. Wilson." Although it was his typical response, this time, I thought the reminder of who he was supposed to be wasn't for my benefit.

Typically, this was when I'd give up. When I'd give into the box he'd locked me in. But I was already a drink in, so between the liquid courage and the certainty that this buzz I felt around him wasn't totally one-sided, I pushed my luck.

"Okay, Mr. Wilson. You can buy me a drink for trying to kill my vibe."

I latched on to his arm to pull him toward the bar. The second my hand touched his exposed skin, the air went from that tingle of attraction to heavy with something more.

His corded forearm bunched, but otherwise, he was frozen. When I looked up to his face, he was fixated on the place where our bodies were connected. Slowly, he dragged his gaze up my arm, and when he paused at the neckline of my strapless black dress, I fought the shiver that tried to race down my spine. There was no stopping the pounding in my chest, though. And it only increased when he continued up my neck to my mouth. With his teeth pressed into his bottom lip, he shifted a bit closer.

Holy shit. My best friend's father was about to kiss me.

The idea burned through my system like wildfire.

But between one blink and the next, a switch flipped and the heat in his eyes vanished.

Swallowing thickly, he spun toward the bar. I was still holding on to his arm, so I moved too.

"You're playing with fire, baby girl."

The words left his lips in a growl, like he was trying to convince himself to think of me as an off-limits teenage girl rather than a thirty-year-old woman.

"I'm not a child," I snapped.

"Trust me, I'm entirely too aware of that." Sidling up to the bar, he gave it a tap with two fingers. "Can I get a scotch on the rocks and a cranberry mimosa?"

With a nod, the bartender moved for the scotch.

"You've been watching me, Daddy Wilson." I'd set my champagne flute down a while ago, and yet he knew what I was drinking.

He leaned in close, his nose almost brushing my jaw.

"Years, Wren. I've been watching you for years." His breath danced over my ear, and my heart skipped a beat. Snapping straight, he yanked his glass off the bar. "Have a good night."

It might have been a month ago, but every moment of that interaction was so vivid in my mind, it felt like yesterday.

Despite all that, this weekend was not the time to needle him. Because this was business.

For a single heartbeat after my eyes met his on the airplane, I'd been shocked. But the clues clicked into place quickly. Not only had he been passionate about *Stonehenge* when we'd discussed it forever ago, but he'd always been a fan of the arts. My first trip to the Boston Museum of Fine Arts was courtesy of Tom. Avery had been bored out of her mind, but sixteen-year-old me had listened to him talk about how art could tell entire stories in one beat of time. I had been fascinated. Part of my awe that day was because he was this cool star athlete I had a massive crush on, but another large part was caused by his passion for each watercolor.

As I turned away from the concierge, his bright eyes locked on to me, making it harder to breathe. Typically he didn't meet my eyes. Or look at me much at all. Today, though, he wasn't avoiding me, and the intensity of his stare had me on edge.

"Ready?" I asked, trying not to wince at the crack in my voice.

"That was quick." His words were low and his lips hardly moved.

The gruff tone somehow felt like a compliment and sent a thrill up my spine.

"I called this morning and requested the room be ready early, and then I checked in on the mobile app on the way over." I knew Tom well enough to know he hated wasting time.

"Well done." His mouth twitched like maybe he was happy, but since the man never smiled, it was impossible to tell. He held out an arm, gesturing to the elevator.

Quickly, I headed that way, and as luck would have it, we stepped right on. The silence in the small stainless-steel box was surprisingly comfortable. Normally I'd try to fill the void with words, but Tom hated nonsense, and the knowledge that he didn't expect conversation put me at ease.

When the doors opened, he held them in place and waited for me to exit before stepping out behind me. I wasn't short by any means, but I felt small when this well over six-foot-tall man hovered behind me.

I pulled my shoulders back as I moved toward the suite door. Normally professionalism came easy to me. I boxed clients into spaces that kept them at arm's length. With Tom, though, that routine was much harder.

Erin's warning ran through my head as we made our way down the hall. When she'd given it, I'd been lost and maybe a little offended. I wasn't the type of person who needed a reminder like that. But in hindsight, she was cautioning me, knowing that I was going to spend the weekend with my best friend's father. Her concern was not about a hookup. Not that Tom would ever let that happen, even if we'd shared a few moments and despite the hints of this electric chemistry that arced between us. No, Erin's warning was about balancing my familiarity with him with his preference for working with a distant professional. That was okay. Great, really. Because I desperately wanted to prove I could be that.

I pushed the door open, reining in the awe that consumed me as I took in the gorgeous sprawling suite in front of me.

"Let me know if this isn't acceptable." I waved my hand, feigning indifference, gesturing to the space—a living room and full kitchen flanked by bedrooms and a balcony with a gorgeous view of Central Park.

"We both know it's over the top," he muttered. Though he must have made well over a hundred million dollars between his pitching career in baseball, sponsorships, and during his time coaching the Revs, he wasn't much for extravagance, and he never flaunted his wealth.

I gave him a sheepish shrug. "Sometimes it's fun to be over the top."

Rather than growl in response like I expected, his lips twitched again. "Sometimes." He strode toward the master bedroom and, unsurprisingly, dropped my bag inside the door.

He turned back, a scowl on his face. "You're staying here. No arguments."

Hands clasped in front of me, I nodded.

Tom had a thing about being closer to the exit. In restaurants, movie theaters, hotels, any place that was bustling with people. He always insisted on being between Avery and the door. Being famous, I guessed, could make a man paranoid. Though I could appreciate his need to protect his daughter, I didn't like the way his instinct to protect me too made butterflies take flight in my belly. There was no preventing the sensation, so all I could do was swallow it down.

As I moved past him, my arm brushed against his abs, sending an electric spark through me.

Hissing, he flinched away. "We're leaving in ten minutes," he gritted out as he spun and headed for the second bedroom. "Be ready. I want to be early."

Early was his natural state. In his mind, if a person arrived on time, they were late. In this moment, though, it felt less like he wanted to be early and more like he needed to get away from me.

Swallowing down the dread and disappointment that stirred in my chest, I opened my bag, removed what I needed, and then went to wait in the living room, ensuring I was ready and willing when my grumpy suitemate came out.

I stood in silence, listening to the zipper of his suitcase, and pulled up the text thread I'd created for our driver. As I tapped out a message, a drawer clicked shut. Huffing, I shook my head. Who the hell unpacked for one night? It was one p.m., and our flight out was at seven tomorrow morning. We'd be here for another eighteen hours. There was no way he needed to unpack. But I'd keep my mouth shut. If I brought it up, Mr. Uptight would lecture me about wrinkles. I worked smarter, not harder, so the wrap dress I'd brought for tomorrow wouldn't wrinkle even if I tossed it in a heap and left it that way overnight.

The sound of another drawer slamming had me cringing. This was supposed to be an adventure for Tom. The amount of effort it had taken to convince the owners to part with the piece of art was an achievement on its own. Owning a work as sought-after as *Stonehenge* should be a celebration, not cause to stress.

Once we picked up the painting, we couldn't leave it alone in the room, so if we were going to celebrate, we needed to do it now. Not only was it my job to make this exchange go smoothly, but to make it memorable too. And whether Tom knew it or not, he was going to enjoy today.

I deleted the text I'd typed out and chose a different route. After a few messages, our plans had been adjusted.

Tom's door opened, snagging my attention, and when he stepped out, my knees wobbled.

Holy shit, the man rocked a fucking suit. It was hard to decide which was sexier: the way the charcoal jacket pulled tight across his shoulders or how the crisp white shirt with the top button undone showed off the thick column of his neck.

His Adam's apple bobbed. "Come."

The word sent a shudder down my spine. Though the command was an innocent one, its dual meaning wasn't lost on me.

I could see the scene play out. His fierce eyes on my face as he hovered above me. His hand between my thighs. Toying with me.

My breath hitched, my heart pounding in my ears—

"Wren?"

That single syllable pulled me out of the fantasy.

Tom frowned at me, standing halfway across the room, and waved me toward the door.

I forced down the reaction I had no right to have. Even if we hadn't been thrown together because of business, my best friend would kill me if I slept with her dad. Regardless of the desires he awoke in me, I had to ignore them. I couldn't go there without risking one of the most important relationships I had.

Daddy Wilson
4

"THE *BAR*?" I snapped as Wren sauntered away. Every click of her red-bottomed heels had my attention wanting to shift down. Had me tempted to let the sway of her hips hypnotize me.

I prided myself on control. Every aspect of my life was organized and planned. Except when it came to Wren Jacobs. No matter how hard I tried, I couldn't control her or my reactions to her. And it pissed me off.

"We're celebrating for a few minutes before we leave." Her voice floated over her shoulder, though she didn't turn as she stepped out of the elevator.

"Why?" I scoffed.

Sighing, she spun and crossed her arms, causing her breast to lift, putting far too much skin on display above the neckline of her top. I tried not to swallow my tongue. Breasts were breasts, and while I loved them as much as the next guy, a single pair should not have the power to make me feel like I was having an aneurysm. Clearly, my body didn't agree with that assessment.

With my tongue still out of commission, I responded with a silent scowl.

"It's important to take the time to enjoy this moment. I won't let you skate past that."

I blinked. Damn, she was right. If it had been anyone else, I'd have happily toasted to my newest acquisition.

Taking my silence for agreement, she turned around and continued on her way.

"Did I forget that I agreed to this plan?" I asked as we made our way through the lobby to the bar.

"We're here, aren't we?" Her full red lips lifted in a soft smile.

My stomach bottomed out at the sight of her like this. Fuck. The damn woman constantly ripped the breath from my body. Without slowing, she sidled up to her favorite holiday drink, a cranberry mimosa, and what appeared to be scotch on the rocks. And like the lost puppy I was in her presence, I followed.

"Thanks, Stew." She sent a finger wave to the bartender.

When the man beamed back, my hackles rose.

"Do you know him?" I stepped up beside her and rested my forearms on the smooth wooden surface, zeroing in on the man who couldn't be more than twenty-two. God damn. Annoyance vibrated through me. For as young as he was, he was ten years closer in age to her than I was.

She lifted one thin shoulder, then held her phone up and gave it a little shake. "No. The electronic concierge said Stew would have our drinks waiting for us."

The hulk inside my chest eased back, no longer trying to rip his way out so he could throttle the poor kid. With a sharp inhale, I ran a hand over my face. I had to chill the fuck out.

She shifted slightly closer, and her soft, sweet scent filled my lungs. "This trip must be nerve-racking, but I promise this will be fun."

Smiling, she rested a hand over my wrist just below the cuff of my shirt. The instant her skin met mine, sparks of electricity danced up my arm.

"Just have a drink." She reached for her champagne flute, taking her warmth with her, and held it aloft. "To what is going to be the easiest, cleanest acquisition you've experienced."

Swallowing, I reached for my scotch. Drinking was a shit idea, but if I didn't unclench, I'd never get through the day. "To *Stonehenge*," I said, clinking the rim of my glass against hers.

"To *Stonehenge*," she whispered, her tone full of genuine emotion.

I froze, and instead of drinking, I focused on the way her lips closed around the edge of the glass and the soft skin of her neck as she swallowed.

"It's customary to take a sip after a toast, Tom."

The urge to reach across the space and pull her to me was over-whelming. I was desperate to taste the alcohol off her lips instead of from my glass. To see if she'd whimper when I slipped my tongue into her mouth and devoured her. To swallow every moan she made.

But I couldn't.

So, jaw tense, I lifted my glass and let the burn of the liquor punish me for the forbidden desire I couldn't shake. I swallowed harshly, then set the rocks glass back on the bar top.

"There."

She rolled those dark eyes fringed by the longest lashes I'd ever seen, but she wasn't deterred. With a single step back, she hopped up onto a bar stool, then crossed her long legs.

I surveyed the room, taking in all the men who were watching her. Wren didn't seem to notice the attention she'd garnered. The woman was probably used to it. Everywhere she went, she was most likely lavished with attention.

Instead of sitting on my own stool, I did the opposite. I stepped in closer, erasing the space between us to block anyone else from butting in.

"Can you go over the game plan with me?" Even though I'd placed myself so close I could feel the heat of her body along my arm, I forced the conversation back into a box reserved for work.

"Sure." Nodding, she leaned forward. As she lifted her drink, a piece of hair floated close, and without my permission, my hand snaked out to catch it. With one finger, I tucked it behind her ear. The move caused my finger to skate along the shell of her ear, and she shiv-ered in response.

Her eyes locked on mine, open and willing. And when she parted her lips and swiped her tongue out to moisten the bottom one, my heart pounded and my ears buzzed. We were so close, just a foot apart. Slowly, I forced my focus back to her eyes. The emotion I found there was like a blow to the chest. Deep desire bloomed in their depths as she stared deep into my eyes. I almost gave in, but before my instincts could take over, rationality kicked in, and I remembered exactly why I couldn't. Because I shouldn't. Right?

I cleared my throat and brought my drink to my lips. With another large gulp, I looked away, relishing the flames that scorched down my throat and into my stomach.

"So when we get there," she said, launching into a detailed account of what would happen the second we arrived at the MET.

I listened to every word, but I couldn't look her way. Instead, I focused on breathing and steeled my resolve, putting this gorgeous woman back in the box where my daughter's best friend belonged, where my own friend's daughter belonged.

I was not an asshole, and I wasn't a player. I never had been. When Avery's mother ended up pregnant, she and I got married. I'd been faithful for the four years we were married. Since the divorce twenty-five years ago, I'd had a couple of relationships, but nothing too serious or dramatic. Each ended on relatively good terms, and none of my exes would trash-talk me. Most would claim I was distant. I was not the kind of man who was controlled by desire or passion.

And that wouldn't change today.

"Sounds great," I said when she finished her explanation.

"So…" In my periphery, she pinched the stem of her wineglass and spun it gently between her fingers. "What's next?"

"Next?" I finally let myself look at her, though I moved hesitantly, concerned she'd be angry or hurt by my clipped response.

She wasn't. Her expression was curious, open.

"Yeah." She leaned against the bar, head turned my way. "You can't tell me that once *Stonehenge* is officially yours, your collecting is done." With an arch of one brow, she hit me with a playful, challenging look.

"Of course not. I have a list," I assured her. "If this goes well, maybe I'll share it with you."

I had plans, and it was becoming more and more clear that Larry and Pat weren't the people who were going to make it happen for me. That was something I needed to talk to Erin about.

"Ooh, throwing down the gauntlet?" She smirked and settled back again. "I love a challenge."

"Of course you do." I spun my own glass on the lacquered surface beside me. "What about you? Do you have a list?"

"Of paintings I want to see up close? Hell yeah, I do."

Normally I hated small talk, but as she prattled on about which pieces she dreamed of seeing, I was enthralled. The way her eyes lit up brightened the entire room, and the slight flush of her cheeks warmed me. Even the way her hands moved as she spoke was captivating. She was bewitching. Especially her depth of knowledge of a topic I, too, was passionate about.

"Do you know how big *Water Lilies* is?" I asked.

She lifted her drink and stuck her bottom lip out in a pout. "Since I haven't been to the Orangerie Museum, I don't."

I shook my head, but before my lips could tug up in a smile, I schooled my features. "I'd always heard it was big, but I didn't expect it to be practically as big as a football field, that's for sure."

Sighing, she tucked a hand under her chin and surveyed the ceiling. "That's why I want to see them all in person. Experiencing art in person is so different from seeing it in a photo on screen."

"Yeah, it is."

"Someday I'll make it back to Paris to see them." She spoke the words as if they were a promise to herself.

My heart lurched. Fuck, I had the urge to promise to take her. Show her *Water Lilies* and then *Town Hall with a Flag*. *Apples and Cookies*. I knew she'd love *Young Girls at the Piano*. The colors blended so fluidly in that piece, like liquid air, almost strokeless.

I hated that I couldn't be the person to make her those promises. I had no right to want her.

I wasn't a man who had many friends. I was a workaholic who didn't make time for people. And besides Avery, I had no family left. I was an only child, and my parents had long passed, so my daughter was my family. Alienating my daughter by dating her best friends didn't seem like the play. Even if Avery was moving on with her life. Even if it was getting harder and harder to resist Wren.

My eyes locked on her lips. Was there a world where Avery might understand? Where she could accept it?

Wren pushed her half-full drink away. "We should probably go. The driver is waiting for us out front."

Frowning, I brushed off the ridiculous ideas, and checked my watch, certain it wasn't time to head out yet. But sure enough, we'd been sitting here talking for forty-five minutes.

She popped off the stool, and once again, I found myself following her mindlessly.

By the time we had worked through details and had the painting in hand, I was completely blown away by the woman beside me. The way she inspected the piece of art alongside the authenticators, checking both its authenticity and condition with a cool, level head, was impressive. And she was an expert schmoozer, chatting with the authenticators and the museum staff while stealthily promoting the auction she would be running on Sunday night. And holy hell, the detailing she discussed was so above my head. This woman's knowledge and ability to charm anyone she met sucked me more under her spell.

I'd been to these things before, and Larry had always done a cursory check of whatever I was buying, but the attention to detail wasn't like Wren's. It almost seemed as if she was as excited as I was about the painting.

"Congratulations." She pressed her hands together below her chin and clapped lightly using just her fingers, beaming, as I shook hands with the director who then passed the box across the table to me.

"Thanks." Lips twitching, I ran a hand over the box. The painting was officially mine and in my possession. I'd almost let myself smile, but before it broke across my face, she threw her arms around me and squeezed. As her sweet scent hit my nose, I froze, but a beat later, my body came alive, and I pulled her close.

Her tall frame pressed perfectly against my body, like a yin slotting against its yang. Without thought, I slid my arms around her thin waist and tightened my hold. My hands splayed across her back, as if they'd been made to touch her. Chin tucked, I nuzzled into her hair and breathed her in.

I gave myself the space of two heartbeats to appreciate the way she felt in my hold, because I had to step back.

Releasing her was torturous, but Wren turned quickly, face still lit up like what we'd just shared was a normal hug rather than a life-altering experience.

While she thanked the gathered group, I chastised myself for obsessing over this woman. I'd always known Wren was smart and talented, but seeing her in action had made it all so much more real. And it had made her so much harder to resist.

But I had to douse the fires of this infatuation and put some space between us. Quickly.

Wren
5

AS THE DOOR of our suite at the Baccarat Hotel shut behind me, I watched Tom with a frown. I had expected the man who'd worked for over a year to convince the owners of *Stonehenge* to sell to be ecstatic. Rather than excitement, Tom had radiated nothing but broody frustration the entire drive back to the hotel. He'd alternated between cursing the flurries dotting the sky and glaring at Kline, the security we'd hired to travel with us back to Boston.

"My room. Please." The grouch flung his hand out, gesturing at the closest doorway. Regardless of the *please* he'd added to the end of his sentence, the words were a command for poor Kline.

My stomach twisted painfully as I regarded the scowl Tom wore. What the hell was his issue? For a second back at the MET, when he'd hugged me, I'd sworn it wasn't just my heart skipping a beat. Clearly, I was wrong.

"Thanks, Kline." I smiled at him in an effort to make up for my suitemate's piss-poor people skills.

Tom narrowed his eyes at me as he shrugged out of his suit jacket and draped it carefully over the back of a dining room chair.

In less than thirty seconds, Kline returned empty-handed. "You sure you don't want me to stay outside?"

Normally we kept security posted outside the suite when we were transporting a painting worth seven figures like *Stonehenge*, but Tom had been clear from the start: When moving the painting, security was welcome—he didn't want to have to carry it and simultaneously fend someone off—but otherwise, he wanted them out of the way.

"No. You can leave." Tom crossed his arms, his dress shirt pulling tight across his sculpted shoulders.

With a nod, Kline headed my way. "Let me know when you've made plans for the morning, with the snow and all." His eyes cut to Tom, and he lowered his voice. "And if you need human dinner company."

"Thanks." Amused, I bit back a chuckle.

Kline and I had worked together on several jobs, mostly moving art for auction. He was a nice guy, his wife was great, and his kids were adorable. I knew because he loved to go on and on about them.

"Thanks, Mr. Brown." Kline nodded at Tom and headed out the door.

The second the door shut, Tom spun on me. "What's the deal with cartoon Rambo? Why do you work with him?"

The knot in my stomach tightened. "Huh?"

Huffing, he waved at the door, his glower deepening. Grumpy was one thing, but I'd never let someone—even Tom—treat any of the people we worked with poorly.

"Kline. The man has a name." I stepped closer and regarded Tom silently, waiting. When he finally met my eye, I raised my chin. "We work with Kline and *his company* because he's professional, trained, and incredibly discreet. He knows exactly who you are, yet even alone in a room, he respects your privacy and would never let anything leak to the public. So how about you play nice with our security and admit that you're happy that everything has gone off without a hitch?"

"Satisfied." He pressed his lips into a firm line that made even *satisfied* a stretch.

I bit back a scoff. "Satisfied?" I asked, successfully keeping my tone even despite the irritation simmering inside me.

He nodded, his face a stone mask. "Yes. I'm satisfied with the results."

Of course. Happy was too strong an emotion for the man.

"Well, since you're satisfied," I said, barely keeping the snark out of my tone this time, "should I order room service?"

"No." The single word was loud and clipped.

"No?"

We'd been in New York for hours and had yet to eat. I was starving. It had taken longer to get the painting than I'd planned, but it was worth the extra time to check and recheck every detail. The MET had their own authenticators on hand, but I'd taken the opportunity to watch their inspection and learn more about the details that mattered. It was an interesting process and a learning experience with the kind of quality I couldn't get in any other place without crossing an ocean. Tom hadn't seemed the least bit annoyed while we went through the paperwork. The second we got into the Escalade after, though, he'd donned his annoyance like a winter coat.

"We aren't eating together." Lifting his jacket off the chair, he turned and strode out of the room. With a click of the lock on his bedroom door, I was alone.

It was stupid, the way my heart pinched. His rejection didn't matter. Many times, clients preferred to spend their evenings on their own. I'd never had as big a deal as today's, but I'd fostered a ton of small ones. Hell, this was the first time I'd even shared a suite with a client. So it was ridiculous on my part to think that Tom would be interested in hanging out with me.

Even so, I couldn't help the way my shoulders sagged as I slunk around the sofa and headed for the large sliding doors that opened onto the balcony. The flurries that had drifted around us on the drive back had turned into full-on snow, and huge white flakes dotted the dark sky. What was hardly a dusting had built up to almost a half inch of snow blanketing the city. Since I'd opted not to bring a coat on this trip, I didn't open the door. Instead, I enjoyed the sparkling white skyline from the warm room.

The snow wasn't a surprise. All week, the forecast had called for it. However, the last time I'd looked, it wasn't supposed to really start until midday tomorrow. It had seemed like our early-morning flight would get us out in time to miss most of the weather delays. But it was really coming down.

I pulled up the weather app on my phone, and when it loaded, I groaned. The storm had picked up speed today, and now most of the snow was predicted to accumulate before six a.m. That made the likelihood of our seven-o'clock flight leaving on time awfully iffy. I hadn't gotten any airline notifications yet, but getting stuck in New York with *Stonehenge* and Mr. I Don't Like Sudden Changes in Plans was not my idea of a good time.

Deciding I'd rather be safe than sorry, I opened the United app next and requested a call from the airline. After a bit of begging, I was able to get our tickets transferred so we'd be in first class on the two-o'clock flight to Boston. Then, with a few keystrokes, I locked in a late checkout with the virtual concierge.

Twenty minutes later, the shower was no longer running, but I still hadn't seen Tom. My stomach was growling so loudly I was surprised he couldn't hear it through the wall. If it had been anyone else, I wouldn't have waited around for him. I would have accepted Kline's offer for dinner. He was probably eating alone, while I was standing around, pathetically hoping the surly man I'd accompanied all day would want to eat with me.

What the hell was I doing?

With a shake of my head, I unlocked my phone once again.

> Me: Want to grab food?

> Kline: At the bar next door already. I saved you a chair.

I scratched out a quick note and then left Tom to his own devices.

Daddy Wilson

6

I WAS AN ASSHOLE. Groaning at my reflection, I ran my hand over my damp hair. The second Wren had wrapped her arms around me in what was nothing more than a congratulatory hug, my body had ignited. It had burned with want, with desperation, with frustration.

And I needed an outlet.

I stretched my fingers and snapped them back into tight fists. This frustrating limbo was unfamiliar to me. When I wanted something, I created a plan and I went after it. All I ever needed was patience and a solid strategy. Thus far, I'd found that with enough work, I'd get what I wanted.

Except for Wren. There wasn't a plan in the world that would get me where I wanted to be when it came to her. Every moment in the last year that I'd spent with Wren pushed me to want more. Denying myself the opportunity to hear her voice or make her smile or touch her felt more and more impossible by the day. Like trying to free myself from quicksand, the more I fought, the deeper I sank. Was it so awful to want something for me? The man, not the coach not the father. But Tom.

Was it wrong of me to want someone for myself?

Desire once again burned through me. I could almost see myself sliding my hands up her body as I slipped inside her.

The images flashed through my head, and my dick twitched to life.

I gritted my teeth. I was not fourteen. I had control. It was the mantra that I'd repeated while I'd taken a cold shower, attempting to snap myself out of this mood. Because I was not fucking my hand in the shower because I was horny.

The buzz of my phone on the dresser had me pushing off my bed. Leo's name popped up once, then again. Although I wasn't in the mood, I swiped over to my best friend's message.

> Leo: Poker. My place.

> Leo: Wifey is doing book club and she dropped the kids at the in-laws. I'm a free man for the next four hours.

I chuckled. The asshole had no interest in being a free man. He was just a fucking drama king.

> Me: In NYC, bro.

> Leo: No shit? Work or play?

I couldn't claim I was here for work, because if he was texting me, then he was texting Collin, my assistant coach, for poker too.

> Me: Play

> Leo: Niiice. Hopefully she can pull that stick out of your ass.

> Me: GIF of the middle finger

> Leo: Haha. Enjoy your date. The storm is supposed to be pretty intense. Maybe you'll get to stay and spend another day in bed. Wink emoji

I swallowed, willing the image of Wren above me to disappear. It was no use, and it was soon accompanied by another. This time of her below me, my hands running along her body, my dick sliding between her gorgeous thighs. My cock thickened, throbbing at the idea.

My phone buzzed again, snapping me out of it. With a harsh breath in, I forced myself to focus on Leo's message.

> Leo: Heath just got here. He says have fun on your sex weekend.

I winced. Jesus. If he had any idea who I was with, he'd be singing a completely different tune. But wait. A moment of rational thought managed to get through my sex haze, even if I wasn't here with Wren...

> Me: Those words did not come out of his mouth.

> Leo: Haha. Yeah, I can't see it either.

> Leo: Funny story, tho. He says Wren is there too. Some work trip. He's worried she's gonna get snowed in.

A message from Heath appeared at the top of the screen, and I clicked over.

> Heath: You in the city?

I swallowed. There was no way to count the number of times the Jacobses had helped me over the years. Baseball seasons were long, and Avery had spent countless weekends and holidays with her best friend. Not once had Heath given me shit about it. He was happy to help my daughter. As I should be to help his.

> Me: Leo told me. I'll text her.

> Heath: Thanks, man. Sorry to interrupt your weekend.

Me: No worries.

Regardless of those words, guilt clawed up my throat. Wren was stuck here with me. It was snowy, she was alone, and I was being a douche bag.

Sighing, I snagged a T-shirt from the top drawer of the dresser and pulled on the jeans I'd worn while we traveled.

I'd eaten close to a hundred meals with Wren over the last five years. She'd come over with Avery for Saturday dinners. I'd taken them out to eat. Avery and I had even spent holidays with the Jacobses. So hiding in my room like this was a major asshole move.

I opened the door, and when the lock popped, I winced. I didn't remember locking the knob, but I could only imagine how ridiculous I'd looked as I stormed in here earlier. Hopefully she hadn't heard me do it.

Expecting Wren to be sitting in the main room, I was shocked to find myself alone. Fuck, I really was an asshole if I thought she'd be out here waiting for me. An idiot too, because she was not the type of woman who let someone walk all over her.

She'd been miffed when I'd acted like an ass to Kline. But the easy conversation between the two of them had put me on edge. Here I was, almost fifty, yet I was acting like a jealous teenager.

I locked my jaw. I'd probably need to apologize about that too. Hands on my hips, I scanned the empty room and the kitchen.

The door to her bedroom was open, so I knocked on the frame.

"Wren?"

When she didn't respond, I peered inside, but she wasn't there either. Her bag was still sitting on the floor by her bed and her purse was on the dresser, so she hadn't left the city to spite me for being an asshole.

What the hell?

I surveyed the room, then wandered out to the main area again. Nothing was out of place. It didn't even look like she'd been in here. Every pillow sat exactly in its place on the sofa. The magazines were spread on the coffee table evenly, undisturbed since the cleaning staff had arranged them.

The only thing out of place was the notepad set haphazardly on the counter. Brow cocked, I picked it up.

Next door grabbing dinner with Kline. If you change your mind and want something, text me, and I'll grab it for you.

Wren

Oh, hell no.

Jealousy bubbled in my gut.

Next door? What was next door? And why hadn't she told me before she left?

That was an easy answer. Because I had ignored her. I'd wanted her to go away, and that's exactly what she'd done. She'd behaved exactly like any professional should have. Yet at the idea of it, anger ripped through my chest.

I turned to the door and stormed out. It wasn't until it clicked shut behind me that I realized I wasn't wearing shoes. Hell, I didn't even have socks on.

Shit.

I shoved the balled-up note into one pocket and dug in the other for my wallet, where I'd stashed the key card to the room.

But my pocket was empty. Shit.

My wallet was on my dresser.

My phone too.

This was the kind of shit I never let happen. I kept tight control over every aspect of my life to avoid this kind of scenario.

And now I was barefoot in the hall and locked out of my fucking room.

I hit the button for the elevator, and when the doors didn't immediately open, I glared at them. I gave it thirty seconds before I hit the button several times in rapid succession.

The stupid elevator was slow as hell.

Finally the light above it lit, and with a ding, the doors slipped open. Inside, I hit the lobby button, followed immediately by the one labeled *close door*. All I could do now was head to the front desk and hope like hell they'd let me back in.

The problem? I didn't have my ID. Even if I did, it still wouldn't do me any good. Not when the fucking room was in the auction house's name.

By the time I got down to the lobby, I was steaming.

"Excuse me, sir," a man called. "We ask that our guests wear shoes when leaving their rooms."

Of course they did. What kind of a jackass walked around barefoot in the lobby of New York's most prestigious hotel? Apparently, my kind of jackass.

I ignored him, heading straight to the desk.

The young concierge's eyes widened as he took me in from my head down to my bare feet.

"I'm locked out of my room." I gritted out the words before he, too, could give me shit about my lack of proper footwear.

Swallowing audibly, he scanned my face, and recognition tingled in his expression. Twenty years ago, everyone recognized me. Between my popularity as the starting pitcher for Boston and many endorsement deals, I couldn't walk down the street without being stopped every twenty feet for an autograph and even sometimes a photo. These days, though, I could move through life undetected most of the time. Die-hard baseball fans would still stop me, and now that everyone had a cell phone equipped with a camera, requests for pictures had become more common. Now, the last thing I wanted was to commemorate this moment with photographic proof.

Remember the time the forbidden woman you were obsessed with was on a date with another guy and you lost it and locked yourself out of your room? Yeah, I'd much rather forget this.

But the young man didn't remark about my shoes or my identity. "Room number?"

"It's 2401," I gritted out, my hands balled into fists at my sides.

He looked from the screen to my face, his lips pressed into a tight line. "Is Ms. Jacobs in the room?"

Seriously? Did he think I'd be standing here if she was?

"She's next door." I turned toward the windows, where the snow swirled, turning the dark night into more of a gray haze. No way could I go out there like this.

He peeked over the counter and pointedly looked at my feet, a brow arched in judgment.

"I'm going to have to call her."

That was fucking great.

Wren
7

"CHASE LOVES it as much as I did. Evie, though, isn't a fan of the long tournaments." He chuckled. "Especially with the little ones. But I think we're in the wrestling world for the long haul."

"As long as Chase likes it." I toyed with a French fry on my plate, but rather than pop it into my mouth, I dropped it again.

My phone buzzed on the bar top. Another text from my overbearing father, I was sure. I'd lived on my own for ten years, but once he'd discovered it was snowing here, he suddenly acted as if I'd forgotten all survival skills. I wasn't even responding anymore. I'd told him I was fine and that I'd rescheduled my flight. He needed to let go. He and my mother meant well, but they needed to let their adult children be adults.

Was this normal? Did parents just never stop worrying about their kids?

Maybe that was it. It looked as though I had another reason to add to the long list of why I had no intention of having children.

"I'll take another." Kline pushed his empty beer across the bar as the bartender approached.

Considering how hard it was snowing, the bar was pretty full. Most of the high-tops scattered around the place were filled with people who'd probably come from the hotel, like I had. It made a lot more sense than venturing out in the storm. We all had to eat, right?

All of us but my roommate, apparently.

I worked to not scowl at my phone where it sat on the granite bar. I'd been stupidly hoping Tom would text and say he'd changed his mind.

Because I just wanted to hang out with him. It was frustrating. There wasn't a single good reason I should be feeling this way. Not to say there weren't tons of bad reasons. Work, my best friend, my parents—all reasons to stay away from the acute attraction that coursed through me every time I was near Daddy Wilson.

Guilt clawed up my throat. I should care that Avery wanted me to stay away from her father. I could lie to myself and say that if he made a move, I'd turn him down, but I knew the truth. I longed for him to make a move. I wished for it. And then felt shitty about it.

I sighed.

"Sorry if I'm boring you with all the kid talk."

Forcing a smile, I hooked my heel on the rung of the backless stool and shifted to face Kline. "Not at all." I'd attempted to make small talk for the last half hour, but no matter how hard I tried, my head was still up in the suite. "I'm just distracted."

My phone vibrated between us, and a New York number flashed across the screen.

My stupid heart skipped as I lifted the phone, but I tamped down on the excitement. It wasn't likely that Tom was calling from the hotel line.

Even so, I was eager to answer. "This could be the hotel." I swiped right and lifted the phone to my ear. "Hello."

The way my heart sank when a young male voice said "Ms. Jacobs" made me once again want to curse myself.

"Yes?"

"This is Henri, the concierge at the Baccarat Hotel. I have Mr...." There was a brief pause. "Mr. Brown here."

Mr. Brown—oh. I blinked.

"He claims to have locked himself out of your room?" His tone lifted at the end, making the statement seem more like a question.

I sucked in a sharp breath. Locked himself out? It was hard to imagine. Tom was not the type of man to lock himself out. Panic seized me, making my chest tighten. Something must have gone awfully wrong for him to have lost control like that. "I'll be right there." I hung up the phone and turned to Kline.

He waved me off, clearly having caught on to my alarm. "Go. I got this. Just let me know if you need me."

Snatching up my wristlet, I jumped to my feet. "Thanks. I'll text you."

I dashed out into the cold, nearly falling on my ass when my heels hit the icy sidewalk. Snow dusted my hair and shoulders in the thirty seconds it took me to shuffle to the hotel entrance, where the doorman greeted me, pulling the heavy glass door open.

As I shivered, I scanned the almost empty lobby, quickly finding Tom glaring at me from where he stood next to the concierge's desk.

Jeans, gray T-shirt and…*bare feet*?

"What happened?" My heart pounded in my ears as I scurried toward him. There was a million-dollar work of art at stake, and I'd acted like a child, letting my stupid hurt feelings take control. I shouldn't have left the room. Shame and anxiety flooded me. How would I explain to Pat and Erin that I was next door at a bar ignoring my job—with the guy we'd hired for security, at that—when a painting worth more than a million dollars went missing?

"I'm locked out." Tom narrowed his eyes at me.

"Do you need me to make another key?" the young guy behind the desk asked. "I just need an ID to confirm first."

I shook my head. "I have mine." And I wanted to get Tom alone so he could explain what the hell happened.

We had been very low-key about what was going on, even with the hotel, because advertising our possession of something worth so much was unwise.

Without another word, Tom turned and stalked to the elevator, leaving me to trail behind him.

"Tom," I whisper-shouted as I jogged to keep up with his long strides. "The painting?"

He stopped in front of the elevator and frowned at me, his forehead bunched. "Is upstairs."

I froze. "You left it?"

Jaw locked, he huffed out a harsh breath through his nose. The elevator dinged, and when the doors slid open, he stepped inside, seemingly ignoring my question.

"Tom." My sharp tone pierced the small space as I stepped in behind him.

Without responding, and with more force than necessary, he hit the button for our floor, which did not take on the warm orange glow the buttons normally did.

The doors slid shut with a whoosh, locking us inside the small space.

"*Stonehenge* is fine?" I asked, hands clutched to my chest. What the hell was going on? Why did he leave the room? No one left a million-dollar painting completely unattended. Not without a reason.

"Key," he snapped.

I pursed my lips. "What?"

He pointed to the still unlit button. "This damn thing needs the key."

"Right." I reached into my pocket and passed the card over. "But what about the painting?"

"It's still in my room."

Bewildered, I swallowed past the nerves rising up in me and gave him a once-over. His hair was disheveled, and his feet were bare. What on earth had made him leave the room, leave his painting, in this state?

"I don't...understand," I stuttered as I pulled out my phone to text Kline and let him know all was okay.

The elevator dinged, and he stepped off, ignoring me completely.

"Tom." Once again, I trailed behind him to our room. Though my shock was quickly fading to annoyance. "Hey," I called uselessly as he pushed through the door.

He stalked across the space toward his room, but I refused to let him shut that door on me. Not without an explanation. Picking up my pace, I stayed on his heels.

The second we were through the door, he froze, and I crashed into his back.

The jarring collision didn't even prompt him to turn my way.

The concern that had held me in its grip dissipated instantly and was replaced with anger. "Damn it, Tom. Stop ignoring me."

Daddy Wilson
8

IGNORE HER? That was laughable. I'd done everything in my power to ignore her for the last five years, and yet I'd been entirely unsuccessful. Every time this woman was in my presence, I was hyperaware of her. Until she mentioned *Stonehenge*, I hadn't even thought about it. Hadn't considered that I'd left it. My entire focus had been her. Was still her.

I whirled around, shoulders pulled back, and threw a hand out, gesturing to the box. "As you can see, it's fine. So—"

"No." She stepped close and poked a red nail into my chest. "I'm responsible for making sure you and the painting get back to Boston, and I can't do that if I'm in the dark. So what the hell is going on?"

The scent of her perfume filled my nose. I locked my hands into fists so I wouldn't pull her closer to get more of the scent that drove me mad. My heart pounded wildly, each beat feeding the chaos that flooded me. I felt like I was drowning, being pulled under by a current that wouldn't quit. I'd fought so hard against for years, and I was exhausted by the idea of staying away.

Her fingertip was still pressed to my sternum. That was the only part of her touching me. Yet my entire being buzzed. I wanted to push her hand away, but that desire was overshadowed by a more desperate need. The need to pull her to me. To make her mine.

My cock swelled at the idea of touching her.

But I shouldn't do this. Because if I let it happen, it wouldn't be just tonight. I knew myself well enough to know if I gave in to Wren, I'd want so much more than today.

"Wren," I rasped, hoping to say something to push her away. I'd done it so many times. I just needed to find the words that would have her retreating. Leaving my room. Saving me from myself.

Her eyes locked with mine. Confusion, frustration, and hurt. Fuck, I didn't want to hurt her. All my resolve fled. I wanted this and I was going to do the work to figure out how to make it happen.

"You weren't here." The honest words flew from my mouth. "And I needed you to come back." Time slowed down as my gaze locked on her lips, full and soft. All I could focus on was how they would taste. How she would taste.

Her lips parted, and she inhaled sharply. Though she was still poking at my chest, the contact was lighter, as if she was considering pulling away.

Holding my breath, I stared at the digit, praying she wouldn't.

"You left *Stonehenge* for me?" The words were barely a whisper.

The moment was too big for anything but the truth. "I didn't even think about it. All I could think about was you." All the good intentions I'd clung to for years were so far gone I couldn't even see the dust of the trail they left behind.

For the space of a couple of heartbeats, I got lost in her wide, dark eyes. The air around us thickened, and when she flattened her palm against my chest, a shiver worked its way through me. Slowly, her hand crept up my pec, causing every muscle in my body to lock. Like the finest silk, the tips of her fingers danced along the skin of my neck. She zeroed in on her thumb where it sat against my pounding pulse point. Every beat pulled me deeper into a lust-filled haze. One that sucked her under too as she shifted an inch closer. Without my permission, my hand clutched her hip and my thumb slipped under her soft white sweater.

As I brushed the soft skin at her waist, her breath caught. "This is a bad idea." The words were barely audible.

"This is a bad idea for so many reasons." I dropped my forehead to hers, desperation clawing up my throat. Having her this close, her skin to mine, loosened the knot in my chest. There were tons of reasons why she shouldn't be mine. My daughter, her parents, our working relationship. I should have stopped this. I should have felt guilty that I needed Wren in this way. "But I don't give a shit about any of them."

She lifted her chin. Our breaths mingled. Our noses brushed. Our lips were so close I could feel the heat of her mouth against mine.

"Tom." The way she whimpered my name shredded the last string of my control.

"If you don't want this, then stop me now," I begged. I'd lost the strength to hold back any longer. The only thing I cared about more than my need for Wren was Wren herself.

Holding my breath, I backed off a fraction, searching her eyes for an answer.

"I want this so badly." With that, she closed the distance and pressed her mouth to mine.

The second our lips met, an inferno lit inside me. Normally a kiss was a kiss. But with Wren, it was branding. A permanent mark on my skin. On my heart. I cupped her cheek and took control of her mouth, running my tongue along the seam of her lips, demanding her to open for me.

She whimpered, but I swallowed the sound down. Instead of giving into my control like I expected, she pushed back. Tangling her tongue with mine. Matching my fervor. Claiming me as much as I claimed her. The power she wielded made my cock throb.

"Less clothing," Wren mumbled against my lips.

I stepped back, releasing her. "Then you better take some off." Running my tongue over my lower lip, I savored her taste. "I want to see you." I dragged my gaze down the column of her throat, over her breasts, then reached out, letting my finger trail the path my eyes had taken. "I want to see the tits that have been teasing me for far too long."

I toyed with her nipple through the fabric of her sweater and bra, causing her to suck in a sharp breath. Then I let my finger trail lower.

"I want to see all this smooth skin." I moved along one hip, then slipped my finger between her thighs.

Heat radiated through her pants, her body quivering. Pride swelled in my chest at how easily I elicited a reaction from her.

"Then I want to see this pretty pussy glisten for me." I slid both hands up her sides now, pulling her sweater with me. I tossed it to the side, and at the sight of white lace, a deep ache throbbed inside me. She was all smooth skin and fierce, needy eyes. Wren was beautiful and young and entirely too good for me. But damn, I wanted her anyway. I gripped her wrist and tugged her along with me toward the bed. When my legs hit the mattress, I stopped. My hands itched to hold her breasts, tease her, play. But instead, I cupped her cheeks and claimed her mouth one more time.

Savoring the press of her lips to mine, I slowed my movements, tangling my tongue with hers, building a fire between us with each spark. I slid my hands to the slope of her neck, letting my fingertips brush against her skin, then dance along her collarbone. Wanting the desire to build slowly in her system, I kissed my way down her throat and over her breasts and stomach until I dropped to my knees in front of her.

Swirling a thumb along her ankle, I lifted her foot to remove her shoe.

Chin tucked to her chest, she arched a brow. "Most men don't like to be the one on their knees."

I fought the smirk twitching at my lips. "Most *boys* don't want to be on their knees, Wren." I reached for her second shoe. "You're not dating boys anymore. Now you've got a man who knows what it is to treasure something priceless." I ran my hands up her outer thighs to her waistband and teased my thumb along the hem until she shuddered. "And don't mistake my position for submission." Angling forward, I brushed my nose along the apex of her thighs.

Her whimper and the scent of her arousal spurred me on and made me throb. My cock was pulsing painfully in my pants, but I refused to rush this. Not when I'd waited years for this moment. More than anything, I wanted to give her pleasure over and over until she fell back, exhausted and sated.

Slowly, I unzipped her pants, then lowered them. When I'd tugged them off completely, I pushed her back onto the bed. At the sight before me, I lost my breath. White lace against her tan, silky skin, black hair spread along the white comforter. I was looking at the most vivid of fantasies.

My body throbbed, but it was my chest that froze me in place. The tightness that I'd been fighting against for so long released. Even in a moment that my cock was trying to beat its way out of my jeans to get to her, just seeing her in front of me settled me.

"You're fucking beautiful, baby girl."

Her mouth quirked up on one side. "So are you, Daddy Wilson."

A shiver raced down my spine, and need drove me forward. Heart pounding, I slipped the lace panties off her body, then kissed and nipped my way up her inner thigh, reveling in the way goose bumps broke out in my wake. When I reached her pussy, I blew a warm breath against her, then kissed my way down her other thigh.

"Tom." She whined, writhing beneath me. "Don't tease me."

"My needy girl." I ran my tongue back up her thigh, the move slow and torturous. Only then did I finally let myself have a taste.

At the tangy perfection of her flavor, a groan resonated through my chest. And as I lapped at her pussy, licking her clit over and over, she squirmed, rocking her hips against my face and clutching at my hair.

She tugged harshly, sending fire licking up my spine and fierce desire rocking my core.

"Oh my God, you're good at this." She panted.

My answering chuckle made her moan.

"Please."

I flicked my tongue back and forth against her, driving her closer and closer to the edge. Her back arched, pressing her pussy hard against me. Her breaths got deeper, her squirms more insistent. Fuck, she was close. Without letting up on her clit, I slipped two fingers into her tight heat and curved them until they hit the spot that would make her scream. As she bucked against my mouth, I pulled her clit between my lips and sucked hard.

"Oh shit." Her scream echoed in my ears as she came on my tongue, yanking on my hair, her legs quivering around me.

Determined to make her pleasure last, I worked her through every pulse, not letting up until her orgasm faded. When she sagged against the mattress, I slowly kissed my way up her body and settled my lips against hers. She thrust her tongue into my mouth, pulling a groan from me, causing my cock to press against my zipper, begging to be let free. Damn, I wished this could go farther.

"I want fewer clothes," she demanded, pulling at my shirt.

I shook my head. "I don't have a condom." Nothing about this trip should have required one. I wasn't a one-night-stand man. I planned things. Sex, until this moment, wasn't something I allowed my body to take control over. I tucked a wayward strand of hair behind her ear and kissed her forehead. "I'm sorry."

She shuddered beneath me. "I'm on birth control."

I pulled back, breath escaping my lungs.

"I'm on the Depo shot, and I'm good." Focus locked on me, she sank her teeth into her lower lip.

My heart pounded in my ears and my vision faded for a moment. "You want me to take you bare?"

She nodded. "I want to feel you inside me." She reached for my shirt again. "Please. I'm good."

Fuck. I hadn't done that since I was married. And the idea of being bare inside Wren? I groaned. "You're going to kill me, baby girl."

Despite my better judgment, I let her slip my shirt over my head, and as she tossed it to the floor, I lowered until my skin pressed against hers. I kissed her again, forcing her back into the mattress, my tongue dominating her mouth the way I wanted to own her body.

"Clothes off," she panted and as she slipped her bra off her arms.

With hands far more shaky than they had a right to be, I hauled myself up and shucked my pants. The second I hovered over her on the bed, she wrapped her fingers around my dick, using her thumb to spread the precum already leaking from the tip. The slow way she circled my crown was pure torture. I locked up every muscle to avoid thrusting into her hand.

When she finally notched me against her wet pussy, my breath sawed in and out of my lungs harshly. The feeling was too much, yet not enough.

Needing to rein myself in, to take back control, I took a deep breath and held back.

"Please. I want to feel your cock inside me."

Feeling a little more grounded, I let out a long breath and guided myself inside her hot body. Her eyes rolled back and her lips parted as she stretched, sucking my dick in deep, inch by inch. At the way my body became part of her, a flash fire ignited and spread through my every cell. Unable to keep my movements slow for a second longer, I pulled back and thrust hard.

"*Yes*." The breathy sound slipped through her lips.

I sealed my mouth over hers as I rutted against her, lost to the kinds of emotions I normally didn't let myself give in to. Thrusting deep, I watched her face, the need and ecstasy in her expression making my chest tight and my lungs burn.

"Your cock feels so good. Oh God. Right there. There," she chanted, spurring me on. Every pound drove her higher. With every stroke, her pussy quivered and tightened around me.

"Come for me," I demanded, snapping my hips in a steady rhythm. "Milk my cock. Fuck, you feel good."

"I'm so close," she moaned, meeting me stroke for stroke.

Stomach tightening and spine tingling, I drove into her without mercy, close to the edge myself but wanting to make this last for her.

Her nails bit into my arms, and her legs shook. "Tom. Yes. Oh God, Tom."

"Fuck." I groaned as she clenched around me. Pulsing over and over. But I didn't stop. I wanted more.

"Again," I demanded, gritting my teeth against my own fierce need. I wasn't ready for the moment to end. I held myself back, desperate to feel her come over and over again on my bare cock.

"I can't," she cried, her voice shaky and hoarse.

"You will." I shifted to my knees, dragging her hips up, angling her just right, and slowed my thrusts, savoring the way she spasmed around my dick with the aftershocks of her orgasm. With one deep thrust after another, I worked, taking my cues from her reactions and shifting slightly until her eyes popped wide.

"Oh shit. There."

She reached for my hips, but I tsked and batted one hand away. I would be the one controlling her body. I would be the one to give her the pleasure her pussy literally wept for.

"I need—" She panted, throwing her head back.

"Tell me what you need, and I'll make it happen, baby girl."

She shuddered, her chest heaving. "I need you to play with my clit."

Without argument, I rubbed slow, firm circles where she needed me most.

Instantly, her eyes rolled back. "How do you feel so good?"

"Because my dick was made to make your pussy quiver."

She clenched around me. Damn, my girl loved the dirty talk.

"Only my cock can make you feel this way. Because—" My stomach tightened, catching me off guard, and my spine tingled. Gritting my teeth to hold back my own release, I sped up, plunging into her hard and fast, still working her clit until her pussy pulsed around me.

Black spots dotted my vision as I rocked into her, drawing out my strokes until they were torturously slow. Sinking deep and grinding my hips against hers.

"Tom," she moaned, coming a third time.

Only then did I let myself go. I came so hard I worried my legs would cramp. But I couldn't stop. The pleasure, the need, the desire all mingled into an inferno of emotion as I filled her with my cum, truly marking her as mine. It went on and on until I was emptied out. Out of breath, out of my mind. Then, boneless, I collapsed next to her, holding her against me.

"You're amazing." With a kiss to the top of her head, I forced myself up. She needed to be worshipped in an entirely different way now, so I slipped out of bed and shuffled into the kitchen.

Warm towel and cold-water bottle in hand, I walked back into the bedroom and was met with wide, confused eyes. She was sitting on the bed with my T-shirt in her hand, as if she was contemplating whether to put it on.

I eyed the shirt and cocked a brow. "That's a waste of your time and mine. I'll just take it off you again." I handed her the bottle of water. "Drink and then lay back."

Her worried gaze dropped to my hands. "You don't need—"

"Yes I do. I'll say it again. You're with a man now. Not a boy." Lightly pushing on her shoulder, I forced her back. Once I'd cleaned her up, I pulled back the blankets.

"You want me to stay in here?" Her voice cracked.

Fuck, the uncertainty in her tone was so foreign. I wanted nothing more than to wash it away.

"If my dick is inside you, then you sleep in my arms."

For a moment, she assessed me, but without argument, she slipped under the sheet. As I settled in beside her, she turned and rested her head on my chest. A peace flooded me as we lay tangled together, just breathing. How the hell could someone so wrong for me feel so right in every way that mattered?

She swallowed audibly, tentatively resting her hand on my abdomen. "Is this okay?"

"This is perfect." I meant it. She was perfect. I wanted her again already.

Though I couldn't see a world where I could have her, I didn't see one where I could let her go either.

I was totally fucked.

Wren
9

AS I DRIFTED INTO CONSCIOUSNESS, I stretched an arm out, searching. Unlike all night long, though, my hand didn't hit Tom's warm body. My stomach sank when all I found was a cold sheet. We hadn't discussed what this was, but I hadn't thought he'd disappear in the middle of the night. Not after his comment about sleeping in his arms since his dick had been inside me.

I sat up, pulling the white sheet with me, and scanned the room.

"No. Two o'clock? Perfect." Tom passed the open door. His attention caught on me, and the corner of his mouth tipped up into the almost smile that I'd seen hundreds of times over my life. "I got to go. Thanks, man."

He sauntered through the door, already dressed in jeans and a sweater, and tossed his phone carelessly onto the bed.

"Morning, baby girl."

The growl of the endearment flooded through me, causing all my uncertainty to flee. I might have hated the *baby girl* the first time he said it, but the emotion in his tone every time those two words rumbled from between his lips made my stomach flip.

Dark hair messy, he crawled his way up the mattress, then cupped my cheek with one rough hand and pulled me down to meet his lips.

My heart skipped when he pulled back slightly and rested his forehead against mine.

"You're up early," I mumbled.

"I wanted to get a NYBoys Taylor ham flagel thing for you."

My heart stumbled. He did not go out and track down my favorite breakfast sandwich in all of New York.

"No way," I whispered.

That almost smile lifted his lips. "Yes way. I know how obsessed you are with them. You've even gotten my daughter hooked and begging me to bring them back for her every time I'm here."

"You always bring them back for both of us." The gesture was one I had always written off. Now, though, it seemed like a bigger deal.

He dropped a hand to my neck, letting his fingers skate along the curve and causing goose bumps to pepper my skin. "I only got one today."

His words burst through my chest. It was silly. He probably hadn't even told Avery he was coming to New York, so I shouldn't read into it. Honestly, though, it was impossible not to.

"And you're lucky they were open. I wasn't sure they would be."

Grinning, I clutched the front of his sweater. "How ever shall I thank you?"

He chuckled darkly, his warm breath sending the hair at my temples flying. "I can think of a few ideas." He shifted to lie next to me, and I snuggled into the crook of his arm, resting my head against his hard chest. "Since our flight was canceled—"

"What?" I snapped up. Canceled? The airlines were going to be slammed. I pushed at the blankets, ready to get my phone and make calls, but he held me in place with one large hand.

"New York is blanketed in a good ten inches of snow." He tipped his head toward the window.

I followed his line of sight and squirmed in his hold. "Shit. We have to reschedule the flights."

Without releasing me, he shook his head. "Already tried. Nothing is going out today and everything is booked for tomorrow."

"Fuck." Holding my breath, I inspected the room, my mind racing.

I was in charge of the auction tomorrow night. Not being there wasn't an option, and I had a ton of setting up to do before it. I'd have to make sure the online auction was locked in and have it run a firewall check, then make sure the caterer was set and the bartender had the right wines.

Tom tightened his hold on my thigh. "Wren." His deep voice echoed through the chaos in my mind. "I know you have to be home. I already called and rented a car. The rental company is dropping it off out front at two. I'll drive back to Boston."

"You…" I blinked, shocked that he knew my schedule and that he'd already taken care of arrangements, when that was my responsibility.

"While we were at the MET, you mentioned running the auction on Sunday night."

My breath caught. I might have said it, but not to him. Had he really paid that much attention to my small talk? I swallowed past the lump that had formed in my throat. I didn't know what was going on between us, but I did know it couldn't last.

I picked at a piece of fuzz on the sheet, attention downcast. "Fixing issues is my job."

A growl rumbled up his throat. "I take care of what's mine."

My heart stumbled over itself. "Yours?" No, I couldn't be. Not really. We'd have to keep this a secret.

He gently gripped my chin and forced me to look at him. His jaw was set in a firm line. "You. Are. Mine."

The declaration flipped my stomach. After last night, it was hard to argue with the statement. I really did feel like his. Like there was no possible way to walk away from him.

I assessed him, working to decipher the emotion swimming in his fierce blue eyes. "What would Avery say?" I whispered. My best friend had been clear about her feelings. She did not want me hooking up with her father. Guilt swamped me, making it hard to breathe. Maybe I should have walked away last night. Maybe I should have told him I wanted him to stop. Yet I was almost certain I couldn't have found those words anywhere in my soul. I craved Tom Wilson.

His nostrils flared, and uncertainty flashed in his eyes. He knew his daughter wouldn't be happy if she discovered that we'd slept together.

My father would be even less so. Tom and Dad weren't as close as Avery and I were, but they'd known each other for decades. There wasn't a world where I could really be his.

Forcing a deep breath into my lungs, I donned the sassy mask I'd gotten so good at wearing over the years. "Guess you only get me in New York. In Boston, I belong to someone else." I batted my lashes.

He growled, and before I could tease him further, he yanked me onto his lap and smacked my bare ass. Sharp tingles danced along my skin, and when he rubbed at the spot, my core throbbed.

"Do not sass me when you're naked in my bed."

Once again, my heart skipped, and warm desire erupted inside me.

"Yes, Daddy Wilson."

That earned me another smack. This time I couldn't stop the whimper that left my lips.

"You have no idea what those words do to me," he rasped, burying his face in my hair.

"Then show me."

He clutched me tight and rocked my hips against his, my sensitive skin grazing the coarse fabric of his jeans.

"Are you ready to thank me now, baby girl?"

Wetting my lips, I shifted and tugged on the hem of his sweater. As it drifted to the floor, I pressed my mouth into the warm, smooth skin of his chest. The man had a body that defied his age, with bulging biceps and solid shoulders. Every swell of muscle turned me on. With a groan, I kissed my way down his eight-pack of abs, then helped him remove his jeans.

As I tugged at the waistband, he lifted his hips, and his cock sprang free.

"No underwear, Mr. Uptight?" I teased.

He grabbed my hair, forcing me to look at him. "It seemed like a waste of time when I planned to spend the next four hours inside some part of your body." He raised a brow. "Are you up for the challenge?"

I licked my lips. I loved nothing more than a challenge. "Always."

Smirking, I turned my attention back to his dick. With my thumb, I traced the vein that ran up the length of it, relishing his thickness and the smoothness of his skin.

His legs tightened under me. "I've dreamed of your lips around me so long." He groaned. "Make it happen, baby girl. I need to watch you swallow my cock."

Obediently, I lowered and circled his wide tip with my tongue.

His responding groan spurred me on, and with a deep inhale, I wrapped my lips around him and slowly pulled him deep into my mouth. By no means was Tom small, and halfway down his length, I was already tense.

"Relax." He gripped a handful of my hair, stopping me from taking more of his cock. The bite of pain as he tugged only added to the desperate need swirling through me.

I teased the tight pull of skin just under the tip with my tongue, and his hips shot off the bed, forcing his cock deeper into my mouth.

"Fuck." He snapped his hips again, and I relaxed against the feel of him.

Eyes watering, I worked to take him deeper. Before I could make much progress, though, he yanked on my hair, pulling me back.

"Spin," he demanded, his eyes wild, his pupil fully blown. "I want you to come on my face while I fuck your mouth."

I shifted, and with a firm grip on my hips, he pulled me around until I was straddling his shoulders.

"Scoot back, baby. Smother me with this perfect cunt."

The dirty words had me shivering and desperate. When I didn't move quickly enough, he smacked my thigh, sending another wave of desire through me.

"Give me that pussy now," he growled. I shifted back, settling my legs on either side of his head. "Look at you," he said, his hot breath brushing over my sensitive skin, "already glistening like a good girl for me."

Shit, I loved his dirty talk. Each word echoed through me, making my body throb.

"Please." I whimpered, pressing my pussy against his mouth. I was torn between wanting him to keep talking and wanting his tongue lapping against me.

"When you're choking on my cock, I promise I will give you exactly what you need." The vibration of his words had me rocking my hips.

"Wrap those lips around me, baby girl, and I'll take care of you."

Tilting forward, I grasped his length and squeezed, eliciting a groan from him. I dropped my head and took him deep.

His pelvis shot up, and I gagged as he hit the back of my throat. "That's it. Take my cock like a good fucking girl."

When his mouth made contact with my center, I moaned around him. He lapped against me, swirling his tongue around my clit, and I shuddered. Fuck, he was good at this. Almost programmed to know exactly what I needed. I ground against his face, and when he slipped a finger inside me, pleasure rippled up my spine. Just like last night, I was putty in his well-trained hands.

"See how good I make it for you?"

God, yes. And I wanted it to be that way to him. So as he worked me over, I toyed with him, sucking, teasing, lapping up his length, and then pulling him deep into my throat. I wasn't sure what was turning me on more, his mouth on me or his cock down my throat. I never wanted either to end.

My legs were quivering, shaking. I was so close. Between the way he worked his fingers into me and his tongue lapping against me, my head spun. I wanted more.

I pressed back into him.

"Yes, smother me, baby." The words were muffled against my body.

I ran my teeth up his length and tugged on his balls.

Beneath me, he shuddered. "Fuck," he groaned. "Do that again."

The second time, his legs shook, and he pumped into my mouth with more force, never stopping the motion of his tongue against me. We were reckless and crazed as we worked each other over. Though my stomach tightened, I tried to hold back, to wait for him so we could come together. But it was no use. Pleasure shot through me, dragging me under. As he sucked hard on my clit, I was lost to sensation. I couldn't stop the ocean that swamped me. I convulsed against his tongue as he worked me through my orgasm.

"Damn, you're sexy when you're coming on my tongue. I could do this all day."

His voice pulled me back from the wave. I wanted to give him as much pleasure as he'd just given me, so I focused my efforts again, sucking him in deeply, then lightly pulling back and toying with the tip.

"I love your mouth. Just like that," he praised.

I dragged my hand lower and gave one more tug on his balls before I moved on, sliding between his ass cheeks and slipping a fingertip between. With a hint of pressure, I eased past the ring of muscle and pressed upward.

"Holy fuck." He bucked hard against me. "I'm coming. Shit. I'm coming."

I worked him through his release, drinking it all down without letting up the pressure on his ass.

Eventually, his massive thighs relaxed against the bed and he heaved out a deep breath. Panting, he reached down and pulled be up next to him. He tucked me against his chest and kissed the crown of my head.

"I don't even know what that was. Holy shit. Wren. You're amazing."

I peeked up at him. "And you're smiling."

A chuckle vibrated through him. "That's the kind of effect you have on me."

The words made my heart flutter, but as badly as I wanted to wrap them up and hold them close, I knew better. This wasn't forever. This was fun, nothing more. "Hopefully your cheeks won't cramp."

With a roll of his blue eyes, he relaxed against the pillow. Beneath me, his heart pounded, tempting me to press a kiss to the hard muscle over it. I gave myself one minute to enjoy what would be the last time I would lie next to this man, then I pushed to my feet.

"Where the hell are you going?" he grumbled.

I smirked over my shoulder. "Someone teased me with my favorite breakfast, and I intend to enjoy it."

He peeked one eye open. "Naked?"

"Clothes are overrated. When I'm at home, I spend most of my time this way." With that, I skipped out of the room.

His groan followed me out into the living area. "You're going to kill me, baby girl."

While I ate, he sauntered out in his boxers, tossed his T-shirt to me, and set to work making coffee. When I mentioned how surprised I was that I didn't have to remind him about the extra milk or sugar, he joked about me having dated too many boys.

He was right. After just a few hours with Tom, it was easy to see the difference. He was setting a bar I wasn't sure any other man could live up to.

Since we had a few hours to kill, I reached for the remote and found the Netflix app.

"What are you doing?"

"Putting on *White Collar*." I quickly scrolled to the picture of Matt Bomer's face.

"What?"

"It's a show." I raised my brow as I hit play, waiting for him to either complain about the noise or tell me that if I didn't get moving, we'd be late.

To my surprise, he just eyed me with consideration, his brow furrowed. Had the man never heard of this show?

With my elbows on my knees, I tucked my hands under my chin and sent him a teasing smirk. "It's the thing that plays on the television, you know, other than news or sports. It's make-believe, with actors."

Shoulders dropping, he let out an exasperated huff. "You're not as funny as you think you are."

"You're wrong about that, old man."

He cocked a brow. And damn, he was sexy. I could tease him about being old, but he didn't look it.

"What is *White Collar*?"

"It's a show about art thieves. You'll love it," I promised with a waggle of my brows.

Gaze narrowed, he assessed the screen. "Doubt it." Even as the denial escaped him, he dropped onto the couch next to me and draped an arm over my shoulders.

"You're going to adore Neil. He makes poor Peter nuts."

"I think I might relate more to Peter." Although the words were gruff once again, he was smiling.

Daddy Wilson
10

"READY, BABY GIRL?"

A moment later, Wren stepped out of the room whose only resident had been the bag I deposited in there yesterday.

I ate up the distance between us and reached for it.

Before I could take it, she stepped back, frowning. "You insisted we didn't need Kline."

Yeah, I had, and when she discovered that I'd bought a train ticket for our security guard and sent him home to DC, she'd followed me around, yapping and cursing.

When Wren got fired up, she was feisty as hell.

I loved it. Her passion turned me on. Most people were afraid to stand up to me, but Wren never had that issue. Surprisingly, I didn't hate it at all.

"We're driving back to Boston, just the two of us." The entire reason I'd opted to rent the SUV rather than take a train was so I'd get a few more hours alone with Wren. The last thing I wanted was some random guy hitching a ride with us. "It'll be fine." I'd keep the car locked.

"So you've told me. However, you should take the painting." She flung her hand toward the box. "And I'll get the bags."

I frowned.

"Teamwork makes the dream work, old man," she teased.

A strange mix of annoyance and desire swirled inside me. "Don't remember you calling me old when you were begging me to let you come on my cock an hour ago."

That had hands-down been the best shower of my life.

Her cheeks flushed, but she didn't shy away. Fuck, she was beautiful.

When I leaned in and brushed my lips against hers, she sighed into my mouth. At the sound, that hard fist that remained locked deep inside me once again unclenched.

"Teamwork, it is," I mumbled against her lips. "But let's get going."

I snaked my hand down her body and gave her ass a light smack.

Smirking, she sauntered past me and yanked on the handle of my suitcase. As much as I hated letting her haul our bags, I didn't mind seeing her black Louis carry-on resting on top of my luggage. They almost looked as if they were meant to be together.

"Are you coming?" As she stopped at the door, she flashed a mischievous grin over her shoulder.

I shook the thoughts from my head. I was being such a schmuck.

If Wren didn't have to get back for the auction, I'd be tempted to stay another day and revel in the opportunity to be locked in this snow globe together.

A world where there were no daughters or friends standing between us. A world where we had a real chance.

But that wasn't our reality. We'd have to go home and deal with the fallout. For now, I pushed the thought from my mind and picked up the large box—the reason I'd come to New York. I had always loved this painting, but after last night, it meant so much more. I was certain that every time I looked at it, I'd be transported back here to Wren.

"Seriously, we should have checked out five minutes ago," Wren called from the hall.

I almost chuckled. I was the one causing the delay, and that never happened.

I never got behind schedule. I'd created routines in order to survive the times when I felt like I was drowning.

Raising my daughter while playing professional baseball had not been an easy task. The schedules I'd put in place allowed me to hold things together for the two of us when everything could have fallen apart.

Her mom was little help. Often, in fact, she made it worse. My ex-wife was well-meaning and loved Avery, but she thrived on chaos. She was the kind of person who loved to drop everything at a moment's notice for a new adventure. The kind of person who didn't appreciate the type of consistency required to raise a child. Needless to say, I did most of the parenting, which felt damn near impossible some days.

But I got through it by cutting out all disorder and sticking to strict routines. Miraculously, I continued to work toward the goals I'd set for myself all while raising a girl who had become an amazing woman.

I lifted the painting, and with a sigh, I left the place that given me the most fun I'd had in years. As I followed Wren to the elevator, I reminded myself that with fun came chaos. And that had no place in my life. Even if, for the first time in forever, I wished I knew how to be a bit less rigid.

I circled through scenarios where I told Avery, or even Heath, that I wanted to give a relationship with Wren a try. No matter how many hypothetical conversations I ran through my mind, I couldn't for the life of me come up with the words that would make my daughter or Wren's father okay with us. We were absolutely treading into chaos. The idea of being nothing more than a weekend fling was a rock in my stomach. But the idea of telling the people we cared about most—ruffling feathers, hurting feelings—and ruining relationships caused my chest to tighten with anxiety. But I didn't want to lose Wren now.

When we got down to the lobby, I headed out to meet the man delivering the rental while Wren checked out. Once the painting was lying flat in the back and I had the keys to the white SUV in my hand, I turned back to the hotel and watched her chat with the concierge through the windows. The sight of her eased the tension in my shoulders. It was nice sharing the burden of responsibility like this. Normally, whether it was with work, friends, or even with my daughter, I'd juggle the checking out, the car, all of it. Because I was the one with the plans. And rarely did I find a person who met my standards when it came to capability.

Yet Wren had her shit together. And there was peace in knowing that.

"Ready?" She dropped her black sunglasses over her eyes as she rolled the bags out the door.

I met her halfway to the curb and took them from her. After they were loaded, I climbed into the driver's seat, finding her already waiting with her seat belt on.

So efficient.

Once I'd pulled out onto the one-way street, we settled in for the long ride.

Her perfume filled the car, and instead of pissing me off, it drained the tension from my shoulders.

"You know you're smiling again." Wren rolled her lips in and tucked her hair behind her ear as she peeked over at me, her eyes twinkling with mischief.

"Always giving me shit." I chuckled.

"I just didn't think you knew how to smile."

"I was stuck underwater, holding my breath." I shrugged. Fighting my attraction to this woman had become a physical pain. Letting myself embrace it? That was easy. "I lived with the tension for too long. Turns out it's easier to breathe."

She blinked and pursed her lips. "That sounds like drowning. Underwater, trying to breathe, only to realize what you're inhaling isn't air? And then you're gone."

A deep rumble of a chuckle worked up my chest.

"That wasn't supposed to be funny." Her forehead creased. "I was serious."

"You're right." I rested my arm on the center console so it brushed hers. "I'm definitely gone."

None of the moments that I'd called this woman mine had been anything but real and raw and honest. But there were so many things in the way of getting us there. We had to move slower than I wanted to. I couldn't come back from this weekend, move Wren into my place, and put a ring on her finger. That would be maddness. I was almost fifty. I was well aware of how hard it was to find a connection that felt as right as the one we shared, but I also knew how to show a woman she mattered. And I intended to teach this woman just how much she was worth.

"You're not dead." She rolled her eyes. "Who knew you were so dramatic." She reached for the radio but pulled back without touching it.

"Is this going to be a silent trip? Please don't tell me you hate music."

I fought back a chuckle. "I don't hate music. You can put on whatever you want." Though I hoped she wouldn't go for the crappy pop shit Avery had always loved.

Surprisingly, she stopped when she found a classic rock station. "I love this song." She turned it up a bit, then sat back and sang along to the chorus.

"You know Tom Petty?"

She spun my way, eyes bright. "I love him. This song's great, but 'Zombie Zoo' is my jam."

A chuckle worked its way up my throat. I wouldn't admit it, but that was one of my favorites too. "Of course it is."

"Don't be so uptight." She went back to quietly singing, this time bopping subtly to the beat.

Unable to resist the temptation, I clasped her hand and pulled it to rest on the console between us. She only hesitated for a second before she wrapped her fingers around my hand.

By the time we were merging onto 95, it was clear that Wren's taste in music was pretty similar to mine. Not only did she like classic rock, but she liked country. She even stopped on a few of the classic stations when she recognized a song. Not once did I wince at her choices.

"Wait, wait. This one should be your jam." Wren reached forward with her free hand and turned up the music.

Frowning, I squeezed her hand. "'Dust on the Bottle'? Really?"

She giggled. "Yeah. Old, but getting better with time. Like fine wine?"

I rolled my eyes. "You think you're cute, don't you?"

Batting her eyes, she leaned closer. "You don't think I'm cute?"

"No." I shook my head.

In my periphery, she frowned, as if she truly thought I didn't find her adorable.

Eager to correct her assumption, I kept my focus on the road and said, "I think you're stunning, intelligent, creative, competent as hell, and sexy as fuck. You're blowing me away, baby girl."

Her sharp intake of breath was loud enough to hear over the music.

Anger flitted through me. Not because of her, but because she was truly shocked by my statement. How was it that men hadn't been praising her for these things night and day? Fucking morons.

I lifted our joined hands and pressed my lips to the back of hers.

When she didn't say anything else, I changed the subject, going with a topic I knew would get her talking.

"Is there anything good coming up for auction tomorrow?" Besides the event where Christian's sister sold a few pieces, I hadn't attended any auctions at the Boston Auction House. But I had the ability to bid remotely.

With a smile, Wren launched into a long explanation that she'd clearly crafted for the patrons who would attend tomorrow. If I'd looked at the email I'd received this month, I'd probably know all this information. But this was not what I'd meant.

"Now that you've gone through all the auction house's lines about the paintings, want to tell me what *you* think?" I glanced over at her, wondering whether she'd claim that she'd been the one to craft the email—that what she'd told me was exactly what she thought—or whether she'd give me her honest opinion. I was hoping for the latter.

"Well." She cleared her throat and shifted. "I worked to get three of the pieces on this block." She rubbed her free hand over her thigh, tempting me to stare at her long legs. Damn, they looked good in those heels. It wasn't often I got to actually appreciate her body. Normally I had to ignore her.

"Road, Daddy Wilson." She chuckled. "Watch the road."

I rolled my lips and arched a brow not minding for one second that she caught me. I liked her knowing I enjoyed watching her. Much the way I enjoyed appreciating a work of art, I enjoyed taking in every angle of Wren Jacobs.

"I'm a multitasker. You can trust me." I fought the smile playing at my lips. "So the art?"

"Yes." With a clipped nod, she tucked a piece of dark hair behind her ear. "An abstract painting by an up-and-coming artist from the Savannah area. I'm not personally a huge collector of the abstract, but mark my words, ten years from now, everyone is going to know who Brice Meadows is."

"Interesting." I wasn't big on the abstract either, but if she thought this artist had potential, then I'd look at it or maybe some of his other work, even if it was only as an investment.

"Then there is a Degas." She frowned. "I'd hoped it was in better condition, but it's been reframed too many times. And," she shrugged, "it's much smaller than I thought it'd be. Regardless, the name alone means it'll sell."

"Would you buy it?"

She hummed thoughtfully. "No. It's going to sell for more than it's worth, considering the condition. Unless you love the work, it's not a good investment."

"Will there be any pieces up that you would buy?"

She ran her teeth over her bottom lip as she considered the question.

"*Bridge of Snow.*" Her words were quiet but filled with excitement. "It's a watercolor. I tracked the original down to an artist in rural Maine. I'd seen a print of it; the blend of colors is amazing. The way that painting makes my heart feel the silent peace of the storm and also the bubbling excitement of a snow day is awe-inspiring." Her cheeks went pink as she gushed. Passion looked sexy as hell on her.

I squeezed her hand and gave her a half smile.

"I can't buy any of them. But if I could, that would be the one."

Bridge of Snow. I locked that piece of information away.

Wren
11

"HOW CAN YOU HATE THIS SONG?" No one hated Britney Spears. "She's a classic."

"Twenty-five-year-old me was literally driven 'Crazy' by my daughter with this song." He smirked, proud of his bad pun.

"Wow, someone has dad jokes," I teased.

His eyes cut to me. "I am a father."

My mouth fell open, and I grabbed my chest, feigning shock. "What? Why didn't you tell me?"

His cocked brow said he wasn't impressed with me. "Does it bother you that I've done the kid thing already?"

"No." Our age difference didn't bother me. If he wasn't Avery's father, I'd be hoping for something more than a weekend fling out of whatever was happening between us. "I don't want kids of my own, so someone who's moved past that point in their life is a nice change." I couldn't count how many times people, even my parents, had tried to convince me that I'd change my mind about kids someday.

He didn't say anything. Doubt lingered in the air. Maybe he felt like he'd missed out on a lot of the fun of parenting because he'd been playing baseball through her childhood.

"Unless I'm wrong and you want more kids." I shifted in my seat as I waited for his answer. The nerves bubbling in my belly seemed misplaced. His answer didn't really matter. But the idea of seeing him with a wife and children someday made me feel nauseous.

As he shook his head, a tidal wave of relief washed through me.

"I barely made it through juggling a child and baseball the first time. There is no chance I'm doing it again. Although I don't hate the idea of Avery and Chris having kids."

"I'm so excited for them to have babies." I giggled. "I'm going to spoil their kids rotten. There will be no chance I'm not their favorite."

"That's my plan as well." His lips pulled up in the corner, and he settled his palm on my thigh. The warmth of his skin against mine had my heart beating just a bit faster.

"Uck." I pouted. "I'll never be their favorite if I have to compete against you."

He squeezed my thigh. "We'll just team up, baby girl."

Warmth settled in my chest at that idea, but I wasn't sure what he was saying. Team up as in help each other be a favorite? He couldn't mean team up as a couple, could he? Being direct and asking him about us was the right approach, but I hesitated. There was a possibility that I was afraid of the answer. And that irritated me. Was it possible to get attached to someone this quickly? I swallowed my nerves and hedged around the issue.

"How come you don't date?"

His brow creased, and I braced for an answer I might not want to hear.

"I don't plan to retire any time soon." His eyes narrowed. "Baseball takes a lot of my time. It doesn't leave room for much more."

"You raised Avery while you played." Was I arguing that he could make time?

He nodded. "Your parents were a huge help. Plus, my mother was still alive back then. I couldn't have done it without her. She stayed with Avery when I was out of town, and when I was home, I dedicated all my free time to being a dad. But women tend to want more attention. I travel a lot even in the off season. I don't need to have to silence calls and deal with a million texts during games and meetings. And I don't want to have to come home to a guilt trip or have to constantly comfort a woman who's crying on the sofa because she's lonely."

I scoffed. "Date someone with a life. A woman who has stuff to do when you're gone and is just happy to see you when you're home."

Side-eyeing me, he smirked. "That would be nice."

"Or get her a puppy to keep her happy while you're gone." I'd always wanted a dog, but in an apartment, it'd be a challenge. Without a yard, I wasn't sure I could do it. "A little chocolate lab with big blue eyes."

He chuckled. "Are you saying I could be replaced by a dog?"

"Probably. Who doesn't love puppy snuggles?"

He shook his head, but he was still smiling. It was so weird to see him light up this much. But it looked good on him—the relaxed vibe, even the little lines around his eyes.

"I'll remember that for next season."

"How's the search for the new closer going?"

"Not great." With a sigh, he slumped into his seat and filled me in on a few prospects and some trades they were working on. "I keep saying we need to put Jasper Quinn up for offers. That kid is nothing but trouble."

"He's wild, that's for sure."

He slid his hand from my leg and rubbed his jaw. "Langfield seems to think we need him, but nothing about his skill set isn't replaceable."

"You never liked him."

Just after he came back from the recruiting trip with the team's upper management, Beckett Langfield and Cortney Miller, Avery and I had dinner at Tom's house, and he bitched about Quinn's attitude the whole time.

He gripped the wheel tighter, making the leather creak. "I don't like chaos."

"Didn't you say that about Chris too?" He'd hated his future son-in-law for most of the first season.

"I didn't understand Chris at first, that's all." His eyes cut to mine for a second. "I'm man enough to admit when I'm wrong."

"I will hold you to that statement." I shot him a teasing smile.

He pinched my thigh lightly, tickling me until I squirmed.

"Cut it out."

With a laugh, he released my leg. "You really think I need to give Jasper another chance?"

I shrugged. "I think he meshes well with your team. The guys seem to love him, and the way he and Winters work their side of the infield is magic."

"I'm aware of that." He nodded. "Am I boring you with baseball talk?"

"Not at all. You know me. I love the Revs. I hardly ever miss a home game." Although a big part of the reason was because I got to see Tom. Tease him. Work for his attention.

For a minute he quietly watched the road, but eventually, he grasped my hand and brought it to his thigh. Then he dove back into his worries for the team for next season. The last hour of the ride went too quickly, and I wasn't ready to say goodbye when we approached my apartment building.

"I'll walk you up," Tom said, pulling up to the curb.

"Are you nuts?"

He frowned, still holding tight to my hand.

"Even if you could escape the ticket, you can't leave a million-dollar painting in a car at the curb."

He glanced over his shoulder and swallowed thickly. "Oh, right." It was almost as if he'd forgotten about his painting again, but I didn't believe that could be possible. "I'll at least get your bag out."

He opened his door and disappeared behind the car. I climbed out more slowly, wishing our time together didn't have to end. I stepped onto the curb and he passed me my overnight bag. When I straightened on the sidewalk and turned, he was there, studying me. He lifted his hand and carefully tucked my hair behind my ear and shifted forward slightly. For a moment, I thought maybe he was going to kiss me. Instead, he froze, his gaze darting one way down the crowded Boston street, then the other, before he stepped back.

"I'll call you?"

The words settled oddly in my stomach. I couldn't tell whether it was excitement that he might or dread that he'd thrown the phrase out with the intention of brushing me off.

"Sure." With a wave, I left him standing on the curb. And it took everything in me not to look back.

Wren
12

Avery: Did you make it back okay, or was the snow an issue?

Me: No, I got home last night. I'm at the auction today.

Jana: That's right. Want to grab dinner after?

Me: I can't. Probably going to be stuck here until late.

Jana: Avery?

Avery: We're going with some of Chris's teammates to the Bolts game. Wanna go?

Jana: Hell yeah. Although with the way those guys are pairing off, there won't be anyone to flirt with soon.

Avery: Even Bosco. You should see how cute he is with Harper. Although Evan might be pissed if he heard that you want to flirt with athletes.

Jana: Evan gets me. He'd just roll his eyes.

Avery: Wren, if you want to swing by after I'm sure Mason has extra tickets. His box holds like a zillion people.

Me: Sorry, just seeing this. The auction was ridiculously busy, but everything sold. Even my snow bridge.

Jana: Emoji of a crying face

Jana: Were you tempted to punch the person who bought it?

Me: It was an online bid, so I didn't have to see them. They actually came in at the last minute and drove the price way up.

Avery: I bet that stirred up some excitement.

Me: Yeah. It was strange. The bidder didn't preregister for the auction, but because they've purchased from us in the past, Erin let them bid. It was so dramatic. You should have seen it. The bidding went back and forth until the online bidder jumped ten thousand dollars and finally ended it.

Jana: Jeez, someone wanted that one badly, huh?

Me: I don't blame them. It's going to be gorgeous hanging on the lucky bitch's wall.

Wren
13

"BYE. I'LL SEE YOU SATURDAY." I waved at Jana and Avery, who continued down the street back to the zoo. Since I hadn't been able to see them this weekend, we'd met for lunch. I was stressed that spending time with Avery after the weekend with her dad would be awkward, but more than anything, it felt good to see my best friend.

Plus, what happened between Tom and me was over.

It had only been two days, but I hadn't heard from him. It was for the best, really, to pretend it had never happened. Because it couldn't be more than a fling. He might not have said those words, but he also hadn't corrected me when I'd referred to it as such.

And I was fine.

The lingering twinge in my chest every time my phone buzzed and it wasn't him would pass. No part of me was a relationship girl. I didn't get attached.

Forcing all thoughts of Tom from my head, I hurried through the lobby. I passed the elevator, since in the winter, the stairs were my constant companion. Running in the park during the winter was pure torture, and gyms were boring, so my cold weather exercise consisted of utterly refusing to take an elevator. I loved heels, and I'd spent too much money on them not to keep my legs looking good. The three flights here were nothing compared to the twelve I trucked up and down at my own place. Two minutes later, I was pushing through the door into the hallway.

Pat peeked his head out of his office as I walked past. "Erin wants you."

With a nod, I headed past my tiny space to the huge corner office that belonged to the head of the auction house.

The door was cracked open, and Erin's laughter filtered out. Through the small opening, I could see her sitting in one of the chairs. Rarely did she step out from behind her desk when she conducted business. She claimed the view of her with the skyline in the background intimidated people and kept them on their toes, just where she wanted them. It was weird to see her so familiar with someone.

"No. I'm not angry at all. I absolutely adore this." Her tone was friendlier than normal too. I could almost swear it was flirty as she patted a denim-clad leg.

I tried to fight the smirk forming on my lips. *Interesting.* Erin never flaunted a boyfriend, so this was going to be fun.

Shoulders pulled back, I tapped lightly on the doorframe.

"Yes?" Her attention shifted my way.

I pushed the door open, and instantly, I zeroed in on the broad shoulders and familiar light brown hair.

Tom twisted, and his blue eyes met mine for one beat before he turned away. My stomach sank as the tingle of shock worked its way through my system.

Erin was flirting with Tom.

Fuck.

I blinked.

My boss and Tom? For a moment, I was worried my lunch would make a reappearance and ruin my shoes, but I couldn't have a reaction. And honestly, she was better suited for him anyway. She was in her mid-forties and divorced, and her son was in his third year at Boston College. They were in the same era of life. And she was exactly the kind of woman I'd suggested Tom should find two days ago. She was busy enough that she wouldn't cling to Tom and drive him crazy when he was working. She was smart and gorgeous and stylish, and all of a sudden, I hated her. This woman I'd idolized for years.

Swallowing all of it down, I wiped my hands on my pencil skirt and stood calmly at the door.

"Pat said you wanted to see me." I couldn't stand the thought of looking at Tom, so I kept my eyes on Erin.

My boss hopped out of the chair she'd been sitting in and waved me over. "Have a seat."

I moved into the room, past the bookshelves lined with pottery, small pieces of framed art, and small knickknacks—all things she'd collected over the years. This was something else I aspired to have someday—souvenirs from all my travels. But I could hardly focus on anything at the moment. My brain was frozen on the image of Erin's hand on Tom's leg. Tom's hand dropping to pat it once. The connection.

Chest burning, I took a breath through my nose and forced the emotion away.

I sat carefully, unsure what my role was.

Erin propped herself up against her desk, her legs out in front of her so they were almost between Tom's.

My chest pinched at the obvious intimacy between the two of them. I'd never known them to date, but that didn't mean anything. I knew nothing about my boss's social life or that of my best friend's father's. Apart from this weekend, when he'd been sleeping with me.

Internally, I chastised myself for getting hung up on him. I did not fixate on hookups like this. I typically had no trouble moving on.

So why was I sitting here picturing clawing her eyes out?

Forcing myself to maintain perfect posture, I tucked my hands in my lap. Tom kept his gaze on the woman across from him, almost like I wasn't in the room. My stomach churned, and apprehension rose in my throat.

Get it together.

How would I ever interact with this man again? Unprofessional and immature wouldn't fly. That wasn't who I was, so I cleared my throat.

"What can I do for you, Erin?" I forced a smile.

"You did a great job this weekend. We talked a little about that this morning." She dropped her arms and grasped the edge of her desk on either side of her hips. "Even with all the last-minute changes of plans, the professionalism you showed while taking over this assignment has been evident."

I fought a wince. God, if she knew that I'd slept with a client, she definitely wouldn't be praising me like this.

"However..." She looked at Tom, who sat back in his chair and crossed his arms. "There is something we want to discuss."

Stomach dropping, I swallowed. "Okay." I looked between the two.

Erin seemed like her normal self, but Tom wouldn't even look at me. He hadn't told her about us, had he? No. He had no reason to. So what the hell?

"Pat's been limiting your new clients."

"Uh." That was true. "Yes." I wanted to expand my skill base. Taking on our VIPs had been part of my job for the last three years, but I wanted to track down the art and run the auctions. Even borrow art from the museums and artists for private viewing parties. I wanted to run a gallery or an auction house someday. Not just scour the world for art for my own clients. So I'd asked to diversify. I wanted the big fish.

"I know you've been shrinking your client list, but I'm going to request you take on a new one. Tom has plans, and we'd like you to help him make them happen." She beamed at him, her smile far too bright.

And why wouldn't it be? I'd teased him about being an old bottle of wine, and it was the honest truth. The man had aged well. He was sexy, sophisticated, rich, smart, and fucking incredible in bed. The full package.

Jealousy inched up my spine, but I forced it down again.

Erin clearly wanted me to take this job, but did Tom? It was hard to think that could be the case when he wouldn't even fucking look at me. At first it had been upsetting, but now I was just mad.

I'd wanted this account before I knew the identity of the client. Tom Wilson was the type of VIP I'd dreamed of working with. Larry complained about how often he bought and sold for Mr. Brown, but he was exactly the type of collector I wanted. The type who was looking for high-end art. I'd be a dumbass to give it up even if Tom and Erin were involved.

For a moment in time over the weekend, I thought maybe there was something between us. But I had goals, and there was no way in hell I'd let a fling mess them up. This account would boost me, and that was what mattered.

Beside me, Tom was scowling at his shoes.

Careful to school my expression, I turned to my boss and pulled my shoulders back. "I'm happy to help you, Erin."

"Me," Tom barked.

Both Erin and I jumped at the tone, and I snapped his way, finding him glaring.

"You'll be helping me."

They were the first words he'd uttered since I'd walked into the room, and of course we were back to the snappy demands.

I was over it.

"After this weekend, I hope I've proved how effective I am." I rose to my feet. I'd agreed, and now it was time to bow out of this meeting. "If you send me the file and plans, I'll get to work."

"Thanks, Wren." Erin tucked her long blond hair over her shoulder, her legs shifting to bump Tom's leg.

His black boot hardly moved in response. And I wanted to punch him.

Professional, Wren.

"Of course." I forced myself to meet the eye of the man still glaring at me. "You have my number and my email. Feel free to reach out with whatever you need."

His jaw tightened in response.

What the hell was this guy's problem?

I turned and headed for the door, only pausing for a moment when my shaky hand landed on the knob. I was fine. I just needed to move on.

Once I'd shuffled out and hurried down the hall to the safety of my office, I forced slow breaths in and out. I was not upset. I was not upset. So why the fuck did I feel like I might cry?

Fuck that. I didn't cry.

With my door shut behind me, I collapsed into my chair and dropped my head in my hands, willing myself to get back to a place of indifference. A soft click had me dropping my hands.

My breath caught at the sight of Tom pushing the door closed and stalking toward the desk.

His bright blue eyes locked on me, and my stomach somersaulted.

My heart wanted to jump up and down and do the happy dance. God, I was an idiot.

"What are you doing?" I asked as he rested a hip against my desk beside me, smelling like spearmint and spice and everything I craved.

"Bringing you the file you asked for." Brow arched, he passed me a thick brown folder.

"It's not on the drive?" We kept all our work on a shared drive. Some folders were password protected, but we kept all our information in one location.

He shook his head. "I refuse to keep my information so easily accessible."

I huffed. "And Erin doesn't care." It wasn't a question.

"She knows I'm difficult." Shrugging, he let out a chuckle. "But I'm also rich."

Normally I found our back-and-forth gripping, but I wasn't in the mood. "I'll go through the file." Attention on my computer, I straightened. "Just leave it on the desk."

Rather than leave, he scooted an inch or so closer. At the movement, I peered up and found him smiling at me. The damn man never smiled, so why was he so freaking happy right now?

"You're cute this way." He dropped the file onto my desk and leaned closer.

"What way?"

"Jealous." A dimple I'd never seen before popped on his cheek.

Hackles rising, I glowered at him. "I don't know why you would think—"

He held a finger against my lips and lowered so our faces were just inches apart.

Though we were close, I kept my gaze downcast.

"She dated my best friend for six years. We're close, but she and I could never be a thing."

My stomach tumbled. And finally, I met his eyes. They were bright and dancing with humor. He dropped his finger from my mouth.

"So kiss me, baby girl," he said, lowering his finger. "Because you're all I've thought about in days."

My chest exploded, and my heart took off in a sprint.

He tilted my chin up and pressed his lips to mine, running his tongue along the seam of my mouth, silently demanding access. As I acquiesced, I arched into him and slipped my arms around his neck. I let myself get lost in his touch for a moment, then broke away. I couldn't look away from him as he ran his tongue over his bottom lip.

Shifting in my chair, I tried to settle the throb that ran through my body.

"We shouldn't," I whispered.

He planted his hand on the desk on either side of his hips but didn't fully move away from me. "I think we're past that point, baby girl."

My breath caught, but before I could respond, the door eased open and we lurched away from each other.

"Oh, sorry." Avery stood in the doorway.

My heart fell to the floor with a *splat*. Oh shit. Holding my breath, I glanced at Tom, who slowly, calmly, looked over his shoulder at his daughter.

"*Dad*?" She looked from him where he was perched on my desk to me in my chair and back again. "What are you doing here?"

Without missing a beat, he stood up to face her. While I was drowning in guilt, he didn't look the least bit remorseful. In fact, he looked happy, which wasn't his normal vibe at all. "Erin finally convinced me to let Wren take point on my project."

The suspicion fled from her face, and her mouth lifted into a smile. "The someday gallery?"

Confused, I tilted my head and assessed her. From the limited conversation I'd had with Erin and Tom, I'd thought I was just taking on a VIP client. I studied both father and daughter. I was used to not knowing all the details of their conversations, but it felt wrong in this instance. I crossed my arms, silently forcing my instincts to settle. Fuck, my emotions were ping-ponging today.

Straightening, Tom squeezed my shoulder. "She doesn't have all the details yet. How about you let me explain them?" He rocked back on his heels.

"I'm sorry to irrupt your art world domination or whatever," Avery said, padding up to the other side of my desk. "But Wren and I got our cards mixed up at lunch, and I need mine for the cake testing that I'm dragging Chris to."

She never dragged Chris anywhere. He happily went wherever she wanted.

Arm extended, she held out my United miles plus black card.

I reached for my purse, the move causing Tom's hand to fall off my shoulder. Though our connection had been severed, he didn't step away.

Breaths coming quickly, I pulled out my wallet. "Sorry. I didn't realize."

I held out the same black card, focusing on keeping my hand steady.

"We need to stop doing this." Chuckling, she took the card back, then eyed her father, who was still standing a foot from me. When she focused on me again, she'd sobered. "Just be nice to dad and don't make him crazy."

I blinked, swallowing down a response. If I said *oh, I'll be plenty nice to Daddy Wilson*, which in the past would have left my lips without a thought, I could make things weird. This was the awkward vibe I'd expected at lunch today, but it had been fine. Of course, while I'd been sitting across from Avery, I had been trying to forget the weekend, not kissing him in my office.

Though I didn't respond, a chuckle rumbled out of Tom.

Avery whirled on her dad, her eyes wide. "Did you just laugh?"

"I don't think I've ever seen Wren so flustered," he murmured. "It's cute."

Avery's brow creased. "Cute?" She regarded me again, lips pressed together. "Wren's gorgeous, but..." She shook her head. "I'm glad getting that painting has put you in such a good mood, but stop being weird."

"It's a parent's job to make their kid think they're weird."

"Well, try to maintain a normal level of weird at the Christmas market tonight, okay?" Her blond ponytail slipped over her shoulder as she tilted her head and eyed her father. "You're still coming, right?"

"Wouldn't miss it," he promised. "Want to come?" he asked, now focused on me.

"I, uh..." My mouth and my brain refused to cooperate to form a coherent response. I needed to get it together or Avery was going to start calling me weird too.

"Wren hates the cold. Getting her outside in winter is next to impossible. She's a fireplace and hot tub in the winter girl." Avery tucked her credit card into her pocket and smiled at me. "Call me if you want a ride on Saturday. Chris is dropping me off, so he'll take you too."

"Thanks," I said, surprised I could get a single word out.

"See you later, Dad. Good luck with the art buying." With a wave, she was gone.

When we were alone again, I let out a long breath and shut my eyes. I'd never felt more uncomfortable.

"I like the hot tub idea. Might need to make that happen." Tom chuckled.

Breath catching, I shot him a glare. "Why did you ask me about coming tonight? There's no way I could go on an outing with you and Chris and Avery without it being weird."

He rounded my desk, then turned back to me. "It'd be fine. In fact, I'd love to make it happen." He clapped, the sound echoing off the walls. "But right now, I have other plans. Grab your coat."

"What?" I stood, smoothing the front of my skirt.

"No questions. Either you come with me or I go without you." He pulled my coat off the hook behind the door and held it out to me.

I could have fought him, but honestly, I didn't want him to leave me behind. If Avery hadn't pointed out my hatred for cold weather, I probably would have agreed to the Christmas market tonight.

That nagging worry tugged at my gut again. Because if I let myself pretend that Tom and I could be any more than what we'd already had, I was setting myself up for heartbreak.

Daddy Wilson
14

RIGHT NOW, I should be panicking that my daughter almost caught me kissing her best friend. I should be riddled with guilt. The absolute last thing I should have done was encourage a situation where I was forced to interact with both Wren and Avery. But nothing about being with Wren felt wrong.

What felt wrong as hell was being without her for the last two days.

Maybe I needed time to prove to everyone that we were right for each other, but I'd make it happen. And part of that was allowing Avery to see me with Wren. To realize that my smiles weren't because of a painting but because of a woman.

I climbed into the black SUV behind the woman who had me tied up in knots and let the driver shut the door behind us. Needing to be close to her, I slid across the leather bench and settled so my leg was resting against hers and my hand was splayed over the dark fabric of her skirt.

I wanted to touch her. Hold her hand. Rub her shoulder. Wrap my arm around her. I craved the feeling of her body against mine.

She pressed her teeth into her bottom lip, but she didn't look away from the privacy screen separating us from the driver.

I, on the other hand, couldn't look away from her. The smooth skin of her cheeks and the curve of her neck where her pulse fluttered. In this moment, with her warm body next to mine, I was at ease. It was surprising, since a relationship with Wren would bring entirely to much chaos to my life.

As strange as it was, my typically tense muscles instantly relaxed when she walked into a room.

And damn she'd looked good when she'd walked into Erin's office, with the tight black fabric of her skirt clinging to her hips and legs and the white button-down molded to her breasts. I was pretty sure my tongue rolled out of my mouth when I caught sight of her. I'd had to avoid looking at her, or Erin's endless amount of shit would never stop.

She'd been trying to set me up with Wren for about a year now. Though I'd been concerned about the age difference, Erin swore it was unimportant. It wasn't until this week that I began to see her point of view.

The leather cracked as Wren shifted beside me.

"What are we doing?" She frowned at my hand on her leg, although she didn't remove it.

I wanted to surprise her and talk about my plans once we were there. But much like me, Wren didn't do well if she wasn't in control. I could only imagine that surprises were not her thing.

"I'm taking you to the Isabella Stewart Gardener Museum."

She sighed. "That isn't what I meant." She pushed my hand away, but I gripped her leg, unwilling to let go. "I meant you and me."

I wished there was an easy solution to our situation. I wanted more of her time, her passion, even her glares, but I wasn't blind to all the potential obstacles in our way.

However, there were some simple truths.

"I'm enjoying the company of a woman I want to get to know better."

Her eyes shot to my face, wide and full of questions.

"Because if we were to give this a chance, I know we could be something special."

She stared at me. Her lips parted like she was going to reply. Instead, she swallowed and shook her head.

"And what are we telling Avery? She almost..." Wren shut her eyes.

"She didn't." My chest tightened at the dread in her tone. "And honestly, we don't have to tell her anything."

Anger flashed in the deep black depths of her eyes, like maybe my response was not what she was hoping for.

"I don't mean ever. But for God's sake, Wren. I don't run out and tell my daughter every time I sleep with someone." I winced at the harshness of my tone. Snapping at her was the last thing I wanted to do.

Eyes narrowed, she lifted her chin. "The difference is that she's my best friend, and I usually do. So I'm not sure this can be a thing."

A retort lingered on my tongue, but I swallowed it back, determined to smooth things over.

"I understand that." Even though my heart took off at a sprint at the idea that this was over before it had even begun. Was it possible that while this felt so right for me, it didn't for her? "If this was just a fun fling for you..." My stomach soured. "Then we can leave it at that."

I lifted my hand from her leg.

"That's not..." Her words trailed off, but I couldn't look at her. I needed a few seconds to compose myself first, otherwise she'd see that my chest now had a gaping hole in the center of it.

"I don't think Avery would understand." She let out a slow breath. "And my parents definitely wouldn't."

A wave of guilt washed over me at the reminder of Heath. I might not tell him everything, but I wasn't sure I wanted to hide a relationship with his daughter from him for long.

With a clipped nod, I locked my own emotions away and turned back.

Her shoulders were pulled back, her fists clenched. She was posed for an argument, but there was no part of me that wanted to fight with her. Three days ago, I'd told her to stop me if this wasn't what she wanted. Now, that was what she was doing, so I'd respect her and pull back.

"We can keep things strictly business, then." Even saying it felt like a blasphemy. "All we're doing is touring the museum so that you have an understanding of what I'm working to build."

She straightened beside me. "What?"

"Your new project." I cleared my throat. "I asked Erin to assign you to my account so you can help me build a collection and find a space to start my gallery."

Between one blink and the next, the woman who had me in knots stepped aside and the businesswoman came forward. "You're looking for a curator?"

For some time, I'd hoped Erin would take the role, but her heart was at the auction house. She loved the challenge that came with buying and selling. The thrill of a good bidding war. She cared little for matching up collections or showing off the art in a setting that could speak to people. Until this weekend, I wondered if I'd ever find a person who loved pieces the way I did. Who was passionate and knowledgeable. Someone I could trust with my vision.

"No, Wren. I'm not looking. I've found who I want." In more ways than one. Even if she wasn't ready for me yet. "So if you're interested, I'd love for you to work with me."

She opened her mouth, as if to speak, then closed it again.

"Erin knows I'll be taking more of your time, especially in the offseason, and she's fully on board."

She shook her head once, scrutinizing me, but she didn't respond.

My heart lurched. An hour ago I was confident that not only did Wren want me but that she'd want this job.

But suddenly I wasn't sure she wanted either.

"I didn't know you wanted to open a gallery." Head lowered she picked at a piece of lint on her skirt. Fidgeting, I'd learned, was a nervous tic of hers.

"Until I get better security, I'd rather the extent of my collection remain between me and a select few people I trust."

"That makes sense."

"How do you feel about curating and running a gallery?" For now, she could do what I needed while still maintaining her position at the auction house, but two years from now, when I was ready to open, she'd be too busy to do both. I'd assumed that she'd be interested in running her own place, but I'd also thought she'd be interested in pursuing a relationship with me, so clearly, I couldn't read her as well as I thought I could.

"That's my dream job." Her voice was soft, but my body reacted as if she'd yelled it. The words buzzed through me, lighting me up from the inside.

I hadn't been wrong after all.

I pressed two fingers beneath her chin, forcing her to look at me. When her dark eyes met mine, the air around us electrified. Reminding us both that this thing between us couldn't be ignored.

"I'd love to do it together. As a team."

"Teamwork makes the dream work." A hint of a smile teased at her lips.

I ran a thumb along her jaw, eliciting a shiver. In that moment, I was sure of two things: Wren was fighting her feelings for me as hard as I used to fight my feelings for her. And that with some persistence, I was sure I'd get to call her mine.

Wren
15

Me: Since we left ISG yesterday, I've been thinking. If you want your gallery in a house type of setting, we should start looking at Beacon Street or Gloucester Street. Those types of places sell quickly.

Daddy Wilson: Good morning to you too, baby girl.

Me: It's almost seven. You can't claim I woke you.

Daddy Wilson: You did not.

Daddy Wilson: But I do agree.

Me: I'll look into the zoning of the area. But there's a possibility we can purchase something in a more commercial location and build a space with a home-type vibe. I'll put out some feelers that way too.

Daddy Wilson: Look at you hitting the ground running.

Me: After walking through ISG and talking about your vision, I'm excited.

Daddy Wilson: Me too.

Me: Did you send me lunch?

Daddy Wilson: You skipped it two days in a row. You need to eat.

Me: When did I tell you O'Hannigan's Green Goddess was my favorite?

Daddy Wilson: You don't need to tell me. I just know things.

Me: That sounds awfully creepy, Daddy Wilson.

Daddy Wilson

16

AT THE SOUND of a tap on my door, I remained focused on the whiteboard in my office. My guys were supposed to be doing their offseason workouts, not bugging the fuck out of me. In the last few days, every one of them had swung by. They'd caught wind that I was headed to UPenn and clearly wanted to put in their two cents. The majority of the team believed Quinn was getting his shit together, but I had my doubts. Still, we weren't looking at the Quakers' first baseman, not that I was admitting that to my guys. But Miller, Langfield, and I were heading to the Keystone State to scout the kid whose slider was on fire.

"I said not to bother me," I snapped as I spun to the door.

Wren tightened her grip on the folder she was holding, her eyes widening. "What a way to greet a girl."

"Shit." I dropped the marker onto the metal ledge and ran a hand over my face. "I didn't realize you were here. I thought one of my guys was back to piss me off again."

Shoulders relaxing, she chuckled. "With that growl, I'm surprised they dare to come anywhere near you."

"Ha ha." I tried not to smile, but her surprise appearance instantly lifted my mood. We were in limbo, where she acted as if we were working together while I acted like she was my favorite person.

Truthfully I wasn't actually acting. Very quickly, Wren had become my favorite person. I wanted to wake up to texts from her and think about her as I drifted off every night, which was pretty much what had happened over the last three days.

"Come sit." I tilted my head, gesturing toward my desk.

Practically skipping in her knee-high boots, she made her way over. Her legs alone were the reason I allowed her to sit in my desk chair. Between the black stiletto boots and the short skirt, I'd probably agree to anything she asked right now.

Beaming, she drummed on the folder she placed on the desk. "I think I found the perfect space."

Brows raised, I rounded the desk and rested an arm on the chair, anxious to see what she'd brought.

"It's an apartment building, and right now, it doesn't look like much." Lip caught between her teeth, she peered up at me, her onyx eyes sparkling. "But the zoning is right, and it's downtown. The best part? It used to be a single residence, so the added walls shouldn't be load-bearing, meaning it'll be relatively simple to remove them."

With a hand splayed on the desk, I hovered over her and perused the paperwork. "It's only a couple of blocks from the zoo." Surprising, yet it would be convenient.

"I know." Her tone was high-pitched and full of excitement. "It's for sale, and some amazing person might have gotten us locked in for a tour tomorrow at nine."

Shit. I hated to burst her bubble, so I did my best to school my expression.

"You hate it?" She sighed, peering up at me through those dark lashes. "Okay, cool. I got overly excited."

I dropped to a squat in front of her and pressed a finger to her lips. "It looks perfect."

Grasping my wrist, she yanked my hand down, and those plush lips formed a small pout. "Don't lie to me."

"I'm not." I chuckled. "But I'm leaving in an hour and a half, and I'll be gone for the next two days."

"Oh." Brow knitted, she surveyed the room, her focus catching on my suitcase where it sat next to the sofa. "Can I go see it anyway? If I like it, maybe we can set up a second showing for next week?"

I expected her to be upset that I would be gone. Instead, she didn't even seem fazed. In the past, I would have been irritated if the woman I dated pouted about my trip, but in this moment, I was sort of bummed she wasn't the least bit sad.

"This works well, actually. I won't embarrass myself by asking all kinds of dumb questions in front of you." Wren twisted in my chair, but I grabbed the arm, stopping the movement.

"Don't ever be embarrassed about what you say to me or in front of me." I cupped her cheek. "I want to know all what you think."

Her lips parted, but she didn't respond. It took her a minute, but finally she swallowed. "Well—"

"Oh, damn," Beckett Langfield, the team owner, called from the open door. "Sorry. Didn't realize you had company."

Wren jerked away from me, and the chair whacked into the desk, sending her reeling forward with so much force she almost fell into my arms. Quickly, she shifted as far away from me as possible without scrambling out of the chair completely.

Frustration bubbled up inside me. "Do you knock?"

The question was pointless. No, Beckett didn't knock. He went where he wanted and did what he wanted, then apologized later. The man might have been full of good intentions, but sometimes his execution was shit.

"Sorry." At least Cortney Miller, the team's general manager, looked remorseful. "The door was cracked a little. We didn't realize you had company."

"I should go." Wren hopped out of the chair, snatching up the papers I hadn't really gotten to look at. "Have a fun trip." She shoved the disorganized pages into the folder, then scurried from the room.

Beckett tipped his chin at Wren, and when she was gone, he turned back to me, smirking. "I caught someone with their hand in the cookie jar," he practically sang. "This is the best news of the week."

Scowling, I pushed to my feet. I didn't want him here, and because of his arrival, I hadn't even gotten to say goodbye to Wren.

"Butt out," Cortney muttered from beside him.

"You saw it." Beckett shook his head. "His heart is taken. That's why he's ignored all the women I've tried to fix him up with."

"Or, like I've been saying, he doesn't want to be set up with high-maintenance women," Cortney pointed out.

I didn't want to be set up with any women, but Beckett never bothered with my opinion. Ever since the team's owner had fallen head over heels for the former head of PR for the Revs, he'd been relentless about giving us all a chance at his type of happiness, whether we wanted it or not.

Beckett's lips vibrated as he blew out his disagreement. "Red-bottom boots, manicured nails, perfect hair. A watch that cost more than mine. Man Bun, that chick screams high-maintenance. Now that I'm finished with Brooks and Bosco, this is my new project."

Annoyance rippled like waves of heat beneath my skin. I better not be a fucking project. I would have to kill him.

Sighing, Cortney crossed his arms over his chest, a folder tucked under his elbow. "Fine. Get it all out. Otherwise I'll never get to discuss Storms."

"This is why you're my best friend. Why I gave you the perfect wedding." Beckett sank onto the sofa and rested an ankle on one knee.

I blinked at Miller for a couple of heartbeats. Wedding. That was right. I hadn't seen the GM since he'd gotten married last weekend. "Congrats."

Cortney's eyes softened as his lips kicked up. "Thanks, man. It's nice."

"You should be thanking me for making it happen." Beckett sat up a little straighter on the gray cushions.

"I should strangle you for last weekend," Cortney huffed.

"I'll tell Wilson the story and let him decide."

"No you won't." Cortney held up a hand, the platinum band on his ring finger catching the light. "You can tell it another time, maybe on our one-year anniversary. Right now, the disaster you created is not what we should be focusing on."

"You're right, Man Bun. Our coach is in love. That's the point." Beckett turned back to me. "I want to know all of the details. Don't leave anything out."

With a deep breath in, I sat in the chair Wren had vacated and rested my elbows on the desk. I met his eyes and waited. It took about two minutes for Beckett to sit back, shoulders slumping.

"Damn, now I know what the guys are talking about. You're scary as duck."

"Ducks are not scary." Cortney's man bun bounced as he shook his head and dropped onto the other end of the couch.

"Can we talk about Storms?" I asked.

"I'd love to." Cortney flipped open his file. "I think he has potential to be what we've been looking for."

Discussing a prospect was usually one of my favorite parts of this job. Today, though, my mind kept wandering back to Wren and the building she'd found. A part of me wished I could skip this trip to stay with her, and that was wild.

Daddy Wilson
17

Baby Girl: Photo of a courtyard

Baby Girl: Photo of a roof deck

Baby Girl: Photo of a spiral staircase

Baby Girl: Do you see what I mean? It has so much potential. I think we could do the circle idea. Starting with the earlier works and spiraling through the floors to more modern.

Me: I love it all.

Baby Girl: I can't wait to show you this.

Me: I'll make myself available any time next week.

Baby Girl: Any time? What if I said Tuesday at 4 a.m.?

Me: For you, I'm always free.

Daddy Wilson
18

I SENT the ball soaring just as my phone buzzed in my pocket. Resting my nine iron against my leg, I pulled out my phone.

> Baby Girl: Are you signing Storms?

> Me: Yeah, hoping to sign him when he graduates in May. I'd do it now, but he's set on the degree.

I'd gotten home from the successful Pennsylvania recruiting run a couple of hours ago. As much as I wanted to see Wren right away, she was heading out to the WAG event tonight, so I'd let Leo convince me to grab a couple of drinks with him and Heath at Top Golf.

> Baby Girl: The really important question is, how does his ass look in baseball pants?

I shook my head. The woman was going to make my brain explode. The thought of her staring at my players' asses made me want to kill them all.

Me: Do NOT check out my guys' asses, baby girl.

Baby Girl: Where is the fun in that?

Baby Girl: Don't worry, Daddy Wilson. You still dominate the best ass category. When you wear the pinstripes, I'm in heaven.

Me: Sounds like the Revs will be wearing a lot of pinstripes this season.

Baby Girl: Lucky me.

I smirked. Pulling back a bit seemed to be working, because she was now flirting with me. Something I didn't mind one bit.

Me: Anything to make you happy.

"Is Tom Wilson smiling?" Leo tipped his beer my way.

Smirk slipping, I tucked the phone back into my pocket.

"This chick must really be something." He glanced up at the screen above us where our scores were listed. "It's not often you duck a shot and then smile about it."

Frowning, I surveyed the screen. Fuck, I didn't realize how badly I'd hooked that one.

With a shrug, I slipped my club back into the rack. Then I skirted around Leo's stool to pick up my beer from the high-top where the guys sat. The nice thing about Top Golf was we had our own climate-controlled box so we could drive balls without our fingers getting frost bitten during Boston winters.

"Is this the girl from New York?" Leo asked.

I nodded carefully as I set my phone on the table. If I got what I wanted, then eventually Heath would realize Wren and the woman from New York were one and the same, which meant everything I said in these moments was incredibly important.

"Your turn, dumbass." I waved Leo to the driving box, hoping to end the conversation.

He stood up. "Just 'cause I'm walking away doesn't mean this conversation is done."

Chuckling, Heath rested his arms on the table. "He's never going to let it go. But you really do seem happy, man."

My chest tightened at his comment. This was my chance to say some things he'd remember later.

"I am. I can't tell you how special this woman is. She's incredibly smart and talented. It makes my day to hear from her, even when she's giving me shit." I took a breath and shook my head. "I honestly didn't know I could feel this way."

"When did you meet her?" Heath lifted his beer to his lips.

I did the same, using the moment to search for the right words. I swallowed and set the beer back down. "I've known her for a long time, but I finally pulled my head out of my ass and realized she was worth the risk and the effort."

My phone buzzed and the notification for a text from Baby Girl appeared.

"Baby girl." With a slight head shake and a smirk, Heath clasped my shoulder and gave it a squeeze. "Already at the nickname stage." He chuckled. "I'm happy for you."

I shut my eyes, not so sure he'd be happy when he realized the woman I was falling for was his daughter. "I'm just hoping it will work out."

"You're up, Heath." Leo dropped into the stool next to me and pulled his drink across the table.

With a dip of his chin, Heath stepped toward the tee box to take his shot.

"Tell me it's not Wren," Leo hissed when he was out of earshot.

"What?" I froze, my mind and heart seizing. I was at a fucking loss for how to respond. How the hell had he even guessed?

"You've had a thing for her for at least two years," he gritted out. "You don't hide that shit from me very well. I've caught you staring way too many times. So again, tell me you are not dating our best friend's daughter behind his back."

I swallowed down the guilt that rose up my throat. Technically, we weren't dating. But I didn't think making that distinction was the way to go here. Honestly, it would probably sound worse. Like I'd fucked her in New York and now she wanted to be flirty friends. "I don't know how to answer that."

"Motherfucker." He shook his head and sank against the back of his stool. "You better know what you're doing. I'm going to miss your ass when you're buried under a par 5 at his country club."

"I have a plan," I mumbled.

The first half consisted of getting Wren to actually date me. From there, I could move on to telling people. So we had time. Hopefully.

Wren

19

"YOU GOT THE BONDAGE SHOES." Avery shook her head as I climbed into the back of Chris's car.

"Did you really doubt that I would?" Smirking, I admired the straps that crisscrossed my foot and ankle. Damn, Daddy Wilson would love these shoes.

I frowned. I wasn't supposed to be going there. Although we'd texted about the property and his new closer the whole time he was gone, I hadn't seen him since the day I'd stopped by his office. The distance left a weird feeling bubbling inside me. It was Saturday, and I'd seen him on Thursday. It had been two days, and already, I… missed him—like, what?

I'd mocked women who sat at home crying while their men were away, but could I become one of those women in the span of a couple of days? No. It wasn't possible.

He'd pulled back after I'd brought up how my parents and Avery would feel. And now we were more like friends. Although I didn't think about my friends naked. So there was that.

I nibbled on my bottom lip.

"You're going to make sure no one bothers my girl, right, Wren?" Chris hardly glanced back as he gave me the chin tilt greeting and pulled into traffic.

"I will always take care of her." My tone was easy breezy, but guilt lingered in my stomach. Because although Daddy Wilson and I were only working together now, the feelings remained. I fell asleep thinking about him every night. I fantasized about his hands and his mouth on my skin. I longed to feel him again. The longing and fantasizing had been a thing for years, sure, but now that it was real...?

"Wren?" Avery was half turned in the passenger seat, looking back at me.

"What?" I blinked at her. Shit. I hadn't heard a word she'd said.

"Chris asked if we wanted to meet up with Jana and Evan after."

Normally I was the one leading the charge when a bar hop was on the horizon, but I could use a good night's sleep. I had a list of art to track down, pages of paperwork for zoning rules to read through, and two more properties to research, not to mention contractors.

And none of that was for my job at the auction house.

I was trying to balance the two, but Tom's project pulled me in more powerfully than my normal work. I would be lying if I said working on the file wasn't also an excuse to text him.

"I probably can't."

Chris cocked a brow and eyed me in the rearview mirror. "Is our little Wren growing out of drunken hookups?"

I scoffed. "Never." That was a blatant lie. I didn't want a hookup. Even the idea made me feel icky. "Just busy at work."

"Okay." Avery nodded. "I don't mind telling her we're bailing. I only planned to go for you."

A moment after she turned to face forward again, my phone buzzed in my pocket with what was most likely Avery's response in our group message.

"Do you remember how to get there? You're sure you don't need me to walk you down?" Chris asked as he pulled up to the stadium.

"The first time I went to the Ground Zero was without you." Avery shook her head. "And you know we won't be harassed since *literally* no one but Revs and Bolts players and us WAGs can get in. We'll be fine."

"Overprotective athletes," I teased, hopping out of his car so they could say goodbye without me.

Once Avery had stepped out onto the sidewalk, she linked her arm through mine as we headed past the security guards stationed at the player entrance. "I want to hear all about your trip. How'd you convince my dad to work with you?"

Now that she knew we were working together, she wouldn't stop bugging me about it.

I swallowed past the trepidation rising up my throat and kept my tone easy. "I was shocked when I found out it was him. A heads-up would have been nice." I narrowed my eyes at her. She and her father were close. She knew his schedule and knew he worked with our auction house. It stung a little, that she hadn't told me he was the client I'd been dying to work with.

Avery shrugged. "I actually wasn't sure he was the one buying *Stonehenge* until he got home. He's so secretive about his art. I rarely know what he's looking at."

As opposed to me, who now had lists. I was the one he talked to about his plan and which pieces called to him. The idea that I might know him best sent elation tingling through me.

"But you two got along?" she asked as we made our way down the cinder block tunnels.

I nodded, lips pressed together, afraid my voice would crack or guilt would have me confessing.

"It's weird how quiet you are about the topic." She sighed as we stepped up to another pair of security guards blocking the door to the bar.

"He's a client." I'd use any excuse not to talk about it.

She rolled her eyes, her blue irises almost identical to her dad's. Then she turned to the large man blocking the door to the underground bar between the stadium and the hockey arena.

The Langfields had set it up for the team only, so the players had a spot to hang out without being bothered by fans. I'd been here last New Year's Eve with Avery and twice during the season.

"Avery." The man nodded and then glanced down at his list. "Wren Jacobs?"

Once he'd checked my ID, he waved us into the space filled with Boston memorabilia. Every inch of the bar was covered with team logos and photos through the years. Even signed jerseys hung above every table. It was like the three Revolutionaries—the Revs mascots—had thrown up Boston merch all over.

"Want me to grab drinks?" Avery asked.

I gave her a nod, then broke off to say hi to Hannah, the Revs' head of PR. She and I had developed a friendship over the last couple of years.

"Hey, babe." I greeted the tall brunette with a kiss on each cheek.

"God, I love the shoes. I swear I'd kill for access to your closet."

I pointed my toe, letting her admire the black straps that hugged my foot and ankle.

"Holy shit, those are like a walking sex dungeon." A familiar blond laughed.

"Wren's shoes will make even the most anti-shoe-fetish person come around. Have the two of you met?" She waved a hand toward the woman in a bright blue dress. "Sara's the me of the Boston Bolts."

I hadn't officially met Sara Case, but I'd heard of her. "And if rumors are true, you're the girl who knocked the Bolts' goalie off his feet, right?"

Sara laughed. "More like the girl making Brooks Langfield crazy."

"One of the perks of being in a relationship." Avery stepped into our circle and handed me a cranberry mimosa.

"How's the wedding planning going?" Hannah tipped her wine at my friend.

The four of us chatted wedding plans for a while. In three weeks, my bestie would be a married woman. We'd done the bachelorette thing back in October before the Revs season ended. That way Chris's offseason would be their time. All that was left on my to-do list was hosting the bridal shower the weekend before her wedding and my toast, of course.

My clutch vibrated, and I flicked it open, spying a text notification from Daddy Wilson. I pressed my lips together, fighting a smile as I lifted it out of my bag.

"Ugh. Seriously?" Avery groaned from beside me. "For the love of God, change his name in your phone."

My stomach plummeted. Shit. I hadn't realized she was peering over my shoulder.

"What?" Hannah cocked her head, her blue eyes bouncing between the two of us.

My heart skipped. Tom never texted anything provocative or crude, but I was glad I hadn't unlocked my phone. Just in case. Or maybe wishful thinking. Because I was definitely wishing he'd send me non-work-related texts.

He'd been open to more between us, but I'd pushed it away. Now, though, I was wishing for more. What was my deal?

"She has my dad saved in her contacts as Daddy Wilson," Avery grumbled.

That was why I'd backed off. My best friend would hate me. She'd made it clear that she wanted me to leave her father alone. And I hadn't.

My stomach soured.

"Why is he texting you anyway?"

"I'm sure it's work related." Swallowing past the lump in my throat, I put the phone back in my purse.

"The man is a workaholic." Hannah smirked at me. "Let's grab a refill, Wren." She yanked on my arm, pulling me toward the bar and leaving Avery and Sara behind.

Once we'd ordered our drinks, she angled in closer, her eyes dancing. "Beckett wants me to set up a team event with the auction house, and he was adamant that all communication should go through you and Coach." She tapped her finger on the granite bar top. "At this point, I'm pretty good at seeing through his matchmaking schemes..."

Panic crested like a wave in my stomach. Beckett had seen us together in Tom's office. Though all we were doing was going over paperwork.

"He's my new client." The words were so lame. I wanted to crawl under the bar.

"Free unsolicited advice?" Hannah picked up the glass of deep burgundy wine the bartender set in front of her.

I nodded.

"First, don't hide what's going on. That'll only make a mess."

Eyes lowered, I glanced away.

"Second," she said, pulling my attention back to her, "enjoy the fuck out of that man. I want all details. I feel like he hides so much behind that growl." Hannah tapped my arm.

I opened my mouth, a denial on the tip of my tongue, but I couldn't lie. "I don't know what it is."

Hannah smiled. "For the record, Beckett is positive that Coach is gone for you, and as annoying as he can be, I've learned not to doubt him or his matchmaking abilities."

I scoffed.

"It's ridiculous, but it's true. The man has a weird gift." She chuckled. "Come on. Let's get back. Oh," she said, straightening. "One more thing. Maybe wait until after the wedding, but then you need to tell Avery."

Nodding, I scanned the room of women. It was wild that both teams had been chock full of single guys until only a year or two ago. Now, their bar was overrun with wives and girlfriends. The best part was that every one of the players' significant others was awesome. It was a group I'd love to actually be a part of.

My stomach jumped at that idea, and I couldn't shake it. The idea of attending events with Tom, holding his hand in public, being the object of his affection, sucked the air from my lungs. I could hardly focus on the conversation.

That was until a haughty, overly made-up woman snuck into our circle next to me and wouldn't shut up. I didn't get what Aiden Langfield saw in her.

"I should set you up with War, then the two of you can double date with Aiden and me." Jill beamed.

War, the tattooed defenseman, was hot AF, sure, and a month ago I might have jumped at that, but…

"I don't know…" I glanced around at the other women, hoping one of them would save me.

Harper, girlfriend of right fielder Kyle Bosco, met my eye. "Sorry, I think she's dating Coach Wilson."

I gasped, choking on my drink.

"When I saw them together, he seemed pretty protective," Harper continued.

Saw us? Holy shit. I coughed, spraying pink liquid across the table.

"Wren!" Hannah jumped back, and Avery whacked on my back.

I wheezed and hacked. How the fuck could Harper have seen us? There wasn't a single moment outside the hotel room where anyone could have seen anything.

"I am not dating him," I snapped.

Harper flinched. "Uh." She swallowed, her eyes shifting to Zara Price, the wife of the team's catcher, who was sitting next to her. "I thought—"

"I don't know why you'd think that." I cringed at the harshness in my tone. Why was I freaking out?

Avery was frowning at me, and Hannah was shaking her head. Normally I'd laugh about something like this. Maybe even make a teasing comment. Shit. I needed to chill, but my heart thumped in my chest and stress bubbled through me.

"Zara's party." Harper stepped away from the table. "You two just seemed…I don't know. I guess I'm wrong."

My eyes flitted shut. I'd forgotten, that night, that Harper had been standing so close, and I'd asked Tom to get me a drink.

"It's…" I shook my head.

"Don't mind Wren's attitude. She's exhausted." Hannah laughed. "She's been to New York and back this week and had to battle a snow-storm to do it. Plus she's working on ten thousand things. The girl never stops."

Harper eyed me.

Lowering my attention, I whispered, "Yeah. I'm sorry."

Avery tugged me aside, frowning. "That was a bit much." She whispered as she glanced around. "I get why you wouldn't want people thinking you were dating a client, but jeez, Wren. You were way too hard on poor Harper."

"Sorry. I—" The truth was I didn't want to be here. All night, my mind had been hung up on Tom. I should have been talking to him, not messing everything up. "I think I'm going to leave."

"Are you okay?" Avery cocked her head, studying me.

I nodded, and once again, guilt turned my stomach. Because there was so much I wasn't telling her.

Daddy Wilson
20

Baby Girl: Tonight went horribly.

Me: What? Why?

Baby Girl: Everything felt weird, so I left the party.

Me: Come over.

Baby Girl: It's almost 10.

Me: I don't give a shit. It could be 2 a.m., and I'd say the same thing. Come over and talk to me.

Baby Girl: Are you sure?

Me: I want you here.

Daddy Wilson
21

I FLUNG OPEN THE DOOR, unsure of what she'd said or what had happened. All I'd gotten from her texts was that she was upset.

This shit should annoy me. I didn't like drama. But at the moment, the only thing I cared about was Wren's well-being.

She stood on my stoop, shivering and coatless in the cold night. Looking gorgeous in her red skirt and strappy black shoes. My dick jumped in my sweatpants, and I practically growled at it. My priority was Wren, so my desires would have to settle the fuck down.

After golf with her dad a couple of hours ago, the last thing I should have been doing was inviting her into my house. But I didn't care what people thought anymore. I realized Avery and I would have to work through this, but I knew my daughter so I knew we would figure it out. Everyone else? I just didn't care.

"Wren?"

"I'm fine. This is dumb. I overreacted tonight." Her shoulders slumped. "The truth is, I'm here because I wanted to see you."

More beautiful words had never been uttered.

I pushed the door all the way open and stepped back. "Come in."

I was thrilled that she was here. Even more than that, I was fucking ecstatic that she'd acknowledged that she'd come just to be with me.

She walked past me and through my foyer, her heels clicking on the hardwood floor. Between the hem of her red top and her skirt, a hint of her smooth, tan skin was exposed. I homed in on it. God, she was gorgeous. I longed to reach out and brush my fingers along her soft flesh.

"Is it okay if we talk?" Wren asked as I followed her into my open-concept first floor.

"Always." I leaned against the back of the sofa and waited.

Moving deeper into the room, past the bookcases, she silently surveyed the space. After a moment, she spun back to me.

"I'm surprised *Stonehenge* isn't in here."

Although I had two watercolors on the wall on either side of my entertainment center and an oil painting hanging above my buffet, none of them held much value.

"Do you want to see it?"

Tucking a lock of dark hair behind her ear, she gave me a once-over, taking in my white T-shirt and gray sweats. My cock jumped as her eyes landed on it. And my heart sped as she licked her lips.

"I'd love to see it."

I wasn't sure what we were talking about. My painting or my cock. Either way, I had to touch her. My control was shredded on the floor.

I stalked across the room, and I didn't stop until our chests were practically touching.

Lifting her chin, she slowly ran her tongue along her bottom lip.

A groan rumbled up my throat.

"What are we doing here, Wren?" I dropped my head so my lips rested against her forehead. "I don't want to do anything you aren't comfortable with."

"All night I stressed about Avery. About what she'd say if she found out about New York. Or what she'd think if she knew that I can't stop thinking about you."

My heart pounded, and desire and fear swirled in my chest. Could I stand it if she pushed me away again?

She ran her hands up my sides, causing a shudder to roll down my spine. The feel of this woman's hand on my body was like nothing else.

"I have all this guilt." She pressed her lips to my neck, and my cock swelled against her thigh. "And yet I want to be here with you. More than I want anything."

Cupping her cheeks, I ghosted my lips over hers. Her soft mouth molded to mine, and a whimper echoed through her.

For days I'd been dreaming of this moment. Longing for the time she'd be in my arms again. And my body burned with the need for more.

Tilting her chin, I ran my tongue along the seam of her lips, silently begging her to open for me. When she obeyed, I tangled my tongue with hers, savoring her. With one hand on her ass, I pulled her close. She moaned into my mouth, and I rocked against her.

I wasn't sure rushing this was the answer. I wanted her body, but I needed her heart more. We needed words before this could go any further. So I couldn't allow the pounding need rushing through me, making my cock throb, to control this moment.

Slowly I broke the kiss and held her to me. Pressed together like this, I could feel her heart pounding and hear the panting breaths as they left her lips. Giving myself a moment to enjoy the feel of her in my arms, I relaxed. Then I pressed my lips to the top of her head and stepped back.

With dark eyes full of confusion, she looked up to me.

"I want to show you my favorite spot."

Her worried expression morphed into a smile. "I'd love to see it."

Hand in hand, I led her through the kitchen to the basement steps. Nothing about the stairwell looked special. In fact, half the massive basement was nothing out of the norm.

"What's that?" Nose scrunched, she studied the metal door in the middle of the wall separating the boiler room from my man cave.

"It's my art room." I stepped up to the keypad and hit the bottoms, then twisted the handle to unlock the fireproof door.

The heavy door swung open, and the light automatically turned on.

"Wow." Wren stepped over the lip of the doorway into the room. "It's temperature controlled?"

I walked in and closed the door behind us tight.

"It has its own filtered air. Humidity control, fireproofing, and low lighting to preserve the art."

Her head swiveled like she was unsure where to look first.

"Holy hell, that's a Rembrandt." She rushed to the far side of the room. "This is amazing, Tom." She took two steps forward and then turned. Stepped the other way and spun again. "I saw the file but haven't had time to read through all of it. I knew you had close to a hundred pieces but..." She turned again, her face bright. "This is crazy cool."

Her reaction made my heart squeeze. I was proud of my two-thousand-square-foot gallery. The downside here, though, was that I was the only one who got to enjoy it.

"I love how you grouped them." She moved to the wall on the left. "These five. The sky. It might be different times of the day, but with the way the sun or moon plays off the clouds, they're beautiful together. Peaceful."

Everything about this room was peaceful. Walls painted the lightest gray, the lush carpet, the lighting, even the armchairs throughout the space. It was meant to calm.

"Oh shit. You have Puff." She pointed to the watercolor Chris's sister had done of my daughter's pet Atlantic puffin.

"I bought it when you first auctioned Gianna's art."

She nodded. "I forgot you got that one."

Silently, she admired the wall, her fingers lifting to her lips, her eyes bright as she took in one piece and then the next.

"Where is..." She spun again, her attention drifting over each area until she found my newest addition. Although most of the room was visible from the door, the walls did break the areas into sections. With her sights set on *Stonehenge*, she moved across the space. "It's beautiful," she whispered as she stopped in front of it.

I stepped up behind her. Unable to keep my hands off her, I wrapped an arm around her waist and tucked her against my body.

"The top lighting. It's perfect." The words were full of awe and barely audible.

Although I'd spent hours staring at *Stonehenge* this week, at this moment, I couldn't pull my eyes from her.

The excitement on her face. The awe radiating from her. My God, she was beautiful.

She turned, looking up at me. "This is amazing."

Although Avery and even Chris had said similar things when I'd brought them down here a few months ago, the simple words were much more meaningful coming from Wren.

"Thank you."

"Are the chairs set up in front of your favorites?" She tipped her chin to one of the many large brown leather armchairs.

"Some."

She nudged me back, and I let her direct me to the seat nearest to *Stonehenge*.

I lowered myself into the seat, and she dropped onto my lap. I let her straddle my thighs before wrapping my arms around her back, loving the way she fit against me.

She eyes tracked around the room one more time before looking up to me. "You don't do things halfway, do you?"

I chuckled. "That has been pointed out to me before."

Nodding, she narrowed her eyes, assessing me. Finally, though, she sighed and rested her head on my shoulder, almost like she was hiding her face from me. She pulled in a deep breath. "I really like you." The words were a whisper, like voicing them made her nervous.

"That's good because I'm crazy about you, baby girl."

I felt her smile against my chest. "So if we were going to try an us?"

Palm flat against her thigh, I caressed her soft skin. "Then I'd be all-in."

She nodded, her fingers toying with my shirt. She remained quiet for so long I was starting to get nervous.

Finally, though, the words I'd been dying to hear left her lips. "I want to give us a try."

I tipped her chin up, forcing her to look at me. Her eyes, framed by long black lashes, met mine, vulnerability shining in their depths.

"Nothing would make me happier." I pulled her mouth to mine.

Wren
22

TOM CUFFED MY NECK, locking my lips against his. Loving the way he felt pressed against me again, I sank into the kiss.

God, I'd missed this. The feel of his hands running down my sides had my heart taking off. It had only been a week, but it had felt like a lifetime since his rough palms had scraped over my body. The physical connection between us was like nothing I'd experienced. It was impossible to resist now that I'd gotten a taste of it.

He slipped his tongue between my lips, claiming my mouth, and as I shifted my legs apart, my skirt skated up my hips. With a trembling hand, I squeezed his length between us.

Groaning, he pulled my hand up and yanked my body closer. And as he cupped my ass, holding me tight against his cock, goose bumps erupted along my bare skin. I rocked once and then again.

"Damn, you're wet already," he muttered against my lips.

Arching, I rubbed my pussy against him, but with so many layers between us, it wasn't enough.

"Fuck, baby girl." With urgency, he ran his lips over my jaw and down my neck.

"I'd love that. Fuck me, please," I panted.

"Patience." His dark voice vibrated against my collarbone. Even as he chastised me for being too eager, he brought his hand between my legs, causing my skirt to bunch higher.

I shifted, desperately wanting him to slide my panties aside and touch me.

As if he could read my mind, he did just that, gliding two fingers through my pussy. Without spearing me, without focusing on my clit, he massaged my wet heat.

My breath quickened and blood rushed in my ears. "I don't want to be teased tonight. I just want your cock inside me. I want you to make me come." I begged, not caring how needy I sounded.

With a chuckle, he pulled my shirt off. "Then let's get rid of all this unnecessary fabric."

"You have more than I do."

He yanked his own T-shirt off in one quick movement, and then it was just bare skin. I ran my hands over his pecs, relishing the prickle of his light chest hair. He slipped my bra off, freeing my breasts, and instantly wrapped his lips around one nipple. Head dropped back, I moaned and rocked against him. But the friction of his sweats just wasn't enough.

"Please," I whimpered, rolling my hips and leaving a wet trail along his pants. "Get rid of them."

Frantically he shifted, lifting me so he could push his gray sweatpants down his legs. His cock, long and desperate, sprung free, bumping against my pussy, teasing me with the tip. With a hiss, I gripped his shaft and savored the heat of him.

"I need you." The words rocked through me as they left his lips, spurring me on.

I squeezed him harder, rubbing a thumb over his crown to collect the drop of precum there. Then I notched him at my entrance and sank onto his thick cock.

Slowly, I slid down his length, savoring the stretch. He pushed up from beneath me, filling me. For a moment, I paused, pressing my forehead to his, basking in the pleasure of being connected so fully to this man.

"Use me, baby girl. Use my cock to take away that ache deep inside you. Make yourself feel good. I need to see you come." His words brushed across my lips, burning through my system.

I lifted up slowly and sank down again, rocking my hips against him. When I did it again, his breath hitched and his body tightened.

"Damn, you feel like heaven." Cupping my breasts, he teased my nipples, sending ripples of pleasure through me.

Every pinch of my nipples, every stroke of his cock, sent me spiraling higher and made the ache stronger. Until it was beating through my system, demanding more. I moved faster, lifting and dropping harder. My breath came faster. My stomach tightened and my legs shook. More, I wanted more.

"I need—"

Before I could finish the thought, he circled my clit, sending me over the edge. All the while, he bucked up into me, working me through my orgasm until finally I collapsed on top of him. Hands cupping my ass, he stood, his cock still buried deep inside me, and lowered me to the ground.

"I need more room." Pinning my hands over my head, he thrust hard.

With my legs draped around his hips, he hit that perfect place deep inside me.

I moaned. "Yes."

"You will come again, baby girl," he commanded without slowing. He was almost frantic now as he thrust, his arms tightening on my wrists, holding them in place.

Over and over, he pistoned his hips, sending me soaring. My ears rang and my body racked as pleasure rolled through me.

He groaned. "The way your pussy grips me when you come is so fucking hot. I never want it to stop. I can't…" His words trailed off as he sped up, desperately rocking into me, chasing his own release. "Wren." Moaning, he sank deep one more time and stayed there, his cock fully seated inside me, pulsing over and over.

Finally he collapsed on top of me, pressing me into the plush carpet. I never wanted him to move. If only we could stay like this, in this moment. Forever. On my back on the floor, I surveyed the room, cataloging the pieces of art. My heart warmed at the memory of his face as I first took in each painting. Like he understood how each painting affected me. I'd never felt this type of connection with another person. And for me, it was so much more than just physical.

He shifted his weight and settled so his body rested alongside mine, and with a hand caressing my arm, he studied me, wearing an intense emotion. One I was feeling too.

"This is good, right?" I asked, suddenly needing reassurance that we were in the same headspace.

He blinked, his forehead creasing. "Fuck. If you have to ask that question, then maybe we need to start over."

A giggle slipped from between my lips. "The sex is better than good," I assured him.

"Damn right," he growled.

I patted his cheek, loving the sensation of the scruff of his jaw on my palm as he leaned into my hand.

"What were you asking, then?" He pressed his lips to the center of my palm, and warmth rushed through me.

This moment was perfect. I was afraid if I spoke, I'd mess it up. The nerves almost silenced me, but if we were going to make a go of things, I had to get comfortable with being open with him. "I meant you and me outside the bedroom. When we're not having sex. We're good, right?"

"Baby girl, I love nothing more than spending time with you." He lifted to his knees and held a hand out. "Let's go up and shower, and then we can watch some more Neil Caffrey."

"You remember his name?" The idea that he cared about my stupid show made my heart skip.

He rolled his eyes. "I might have watched a few episodes of *White Collar* this week."

"See?" I let him pull me to my feet. "I knew you'd love him."

He shook his head but leaned in again to kiss me with the hint of a smile on his face.

After a shower and two episodes, I was curled up in Tom's arms. As boneless as I should feel after our evening together, though, I couldn't banish the guilt that swirled in my stomach.

It shouldn't matter what other people thought of us if I was happy, but life wasn't that simple.

"What's the matter?" His deep voice startled me. "I can hear the wheels in your brain turning, baby girl."

His warm palm ran up and down my back, soothing me.

"I just don't want anything to mess this up."

He tensed under me. "I don't either."

Last week I had been convinced we couldn't keep this between us. But right now, our connection felt new and scary. Like even the smallest bump could throw us off course.

"Would you be okay if we didn't tell people about us yet?"

"I'll wait as long as you want." He pressed his lips to the top of my head. "All that matters is having you here with me."

Wrapped in his arms like this, it was easy to believe him.

Daddy Wilson
23

CHRISTMAS. Avery was four or five, in that prime Christmas magic age, the last time I was this excited about the holiday. For the last few years, I'd dreaded it. Last Christmas, I'd even gone away with Leo's family to avoid spending the entire day with the Jacobses. Since Avery had moved back to Boston after college, we'd spent Christmas with her best friend's family. But spending the day around Wren had been torture.

This year, spending time with her was all I wanted. We'd been together for a week now, but we hadn't gone public yet. With Avery's wedding just weeks away, we'd decided it would be best to wait until she and Chris were back from their honeymoon before we made waves.

I stepped out on to the street in front of the massive house and shut the car door. The Jacobs family lived on the outskirts of Boston in one of the many country club communities. Heath had been running Rapid Falls Country Club since the girls were in elementary school. Before Avery graduated from high school, she and I lived three doors down from here. Looking at the large snow-covered yards, it was hard to imagine I'd had the time to take care of one of my own.

With a shake of my head, I pulled the bags of gifts out of my back seat. I was so much happier with my ten-by-ten yard in downtown Boston. Raising Avery here was ideal, but I wouldn't move back now. I liked my city life.

As I approached the house, my phone buzzed once and then again in my pocket. Before I could check it, the front door swung open.

"Dammit. My husband was right." Colleen Jacobs called from the entryway.

"How's that?" I stomped the snow from my boots on the steps.

"I was holding out hope that you'd bring your girl." She smiled.

Stomach knotting, I shook my head. "I told you it was just me." Inside, I was hit by the scents of wintergreen and roasting turkey.

"But I'm dying to meet the woman who tamed the rake."

With a laugh, I clutched my chest. "Colleen, you wound me. I am not now nor have I ever been rakish."

"I do fear you're both watching too much *Bridgerton*." Heath joined us. "Merry Christmas," he said as he took the bags from my hands.

"Merry Christmas." I kissed Colleen's cheek and slapped Heath on the back. "Am I the last one here?"

"Yes. Everyone's in the back." Heath pointed toward the den.

"Except Wren," Colleen added.

"Oh." I schooled my features, going for vague interest even though every cell in my body perked at her name. "Did she hit traffic?"

"No." Colleen sighed. "She claims she's sick, but mother's intuition says she's dating someone."

I fisted my hands at my sides. Sick? What the fuck? She didn't even tell me. My heart hammered and worry buzzed through my system.

"She did not bail on us to spend time with a random guy." Heath frowned, though his expression was unconcerned. "Even this one." He pointed at me. "Didn't bail on us to hang with his *baby girl*. I can't imagine Wren would make up a story."

Irritation built in my gut. Did he not care about the fact that his daughter was sick?

He shrugged. "It's probably just one of those days."

What the fuck did that mean?

"Come on, Tom, the Pats game is about to start."

I stepped forward, ready to follow him, but stopped abruptly. If I went into that room, I couldn't pull out my phone and check on Wren. And I would check on her. Maybe her parents weren't concerned, but I was.

"Just gonna hit the head first." I slipped into the bathroom, and the second the door was locked behind me, I pulled out my phone and frowned at the alerts.

> Baby Girl: I'm sorry. I should probably have called earlier, but I fell asleep and now you're probably there.
>
> Baby Girl: But I'm coming today. Just not feeling great.
>
> Baby Girl: Sorry.

I pressed her name and held the phone up.

"Hello." Her soft voice was music to my ears.

"What's wrong?" I did my best to keep my voice from being too harsh.

"Nothing. I just don't feel great."

"Do you need me to send a doctor over?" The Revs had two on staff. With the right incentive, I could probably talk one of them into meeting me at her apartment.

"It's Christmas."

"I don't care what day it is. You're sick." And I should be there to take care of her. I tried to pace, but the damn room was too small, so I was just turning in circles.

"I'm not sick. I just don't feel great."

I stopped my stupid spinning. What the fuck did that mean? I ran a hand over my face and blew out a breath. "Baby girl, I'm trying not to freak out, so please explain to me what's going on."

"I thought you might remember, but..." She exhaled loudly. "During certain times of the month, I don't feel great."

Like a sledgehammer, the memories hit me. In so many ways, my Wren wasn't the teenager I'd watched grow up. This Wren and past Wren existed in my mind as two different people, but now that she'd forced the idea into my brain, I did remember. She'd stayed with Avery and me on occasion when her parents traveled, and there had been a day where she wouldn't get out of bed. By the way she moaned and curled in a ball, I'd thought she had appendicitis.

My uninformed male brain had panicked, and I'd been ready to call a doctor, but Avery assured me it was her period. Endometriosis. Every month, Wren spent at least one day in bed. My daughter, who never experienced even minimal cramps, felt awful for her best friend. We'd done many ice cream runs.

"What do you need?" Fuck, I felt helpless. If I remembered correctly, there wasn't much I could do for her.

"I'm just going to lay here and be miserable. I'll be fine by tomorrow night. I promise." She took a breath, and I swore I felt her pain through the phone. After another heartbeat, she added, "Merry Christmas. Have fun."

My gut churned. Yeah, that wasn't likely.

"I'll check on you later," I promised.

"Okay, bye."

After she'd disconnected the call, I stared at my reflection. Dammit. I couldn't stay here. Wren was miserable, and yet she expected me to have fun? Teeth gritted, I scrolled to another contact.

After two rings, he picked up.

"Merry Christmas, bro!" Leo cheered.

"Listen carefully," I hissed.

"Dude?" His tone was much more subdued now.

"Listen," I repeated. "I need you to call me back in ten minutes and claim there's an emergency. I don't care what it is, just get me out of the Jacobses house. And Brenna better be on board with the plan in case Heath or Colleen mention it."

"Uh—"

"Leo," I said, tone dark. "I've saved your ass more times than I can count. You're my best friend. The guy who's supposed to help me bury the body. So this is it. *Help me.*"

He cleared his throat. "Cool. I'll call in ten. In the meantime, I'll explain to my wife that we're gonna lie for you because you've lost your mind."

Blowing out a breath, I straightened. "Thanks for not asking."

He scoffed. "Bro, I don't want to know the answers to any of the questions." With that, the line went dead.

Pocketing my phone, I slipped out of the bathroom, ready to say Merry Christmas to my daughter and then bail.

Wren
27

I IGNORED THE BUZZING, unable to drag myself out from under the blankets. It felt like I'd been run over by a truck, and clearly, a wrecking ball was doing a number on my lower back and uterus.

Most women hated this time of the month, but for me, it was absolute hell. While most could stand and move around the day aunt flo arrived, often, I couldn't. And today was one of those days. I'd taken multiple medications and even had a few procedures, and still, I was miserable too often. Even the Depo shot, which the doctor ensured me would help, didn't seem to do much.

The doorbell buzzed again. Dammit. All I wanted was to lie on a heating pad and suffer in peace. But it was probably some poor Door Dasher with food Avery had ordered trying to cheer me up. Hopefully it was ice cream. Though were any ice cream shops open today? I wasn't even sure my regular grocery store was. If Chris's dad hadn't been at my parents' house with them, my bestie would have left to come here. But she couldn't leave her future father-in-law, so the unfortunate person at my door had been lured out to do her bidding. The least I could do was answer.

Holding my breath, I stood. Then I shuffled across the apartment. I braced myself on the door I'd pulled open a few inches, wincing at the shock of pain tearing through my abdomen.

"Baby girl."

The sound of his voice snapped me out of my misery. *Tom?* He stood in the hall, holding a blue cup dotted with snow in one hand and a large box at his side.

"Is that a peanut butter cup Blizzard?" I shouldn't be surprised that he'd once again plucked my favorite thing out of my brain.

He tipped the cup so I could see the red spoon sticking out of the ice cream mixed with peanut butter cups.

"I can't believe they were open on Christmas." Pushing the door open farther, I stepped back to let him in. As he passed, I took the cup and shoved a spoonful into my mouth. Instantly, the cool cream chilled my insides and soothed me.

He took off his shoes in the entry, then carried the rectangular box into the living room, leaving the spicy scent of his cologne in his wake. By the time I'd locked the door and turned around, the box was propped up against the sofa and he was standing in front of me.

He pressed his lips to my forehead and tucked me in close. "Of course I found an open one. And I brought a cooler, so it should still be mostly frozen."

A cooler? Damn, that meant he'd driven God knew how far just to find my favorite ice cream on Christmas. This man, who normally hated to waste time, didn't seem the least bit bothered.

"How you feeling?"

"Happier now that you're here." The words slipped out before I had time to consider them, and for a heartbeat, I wished I could take them back. Before I could backtrack, though, he squeezed my arms and hummed contentedly.

"Me too. I'm happier when I'm with you."

A sharp ache radiated through my back, and I winced. My instinct was to pull my legs to my chest, but that was impossible while standing. Tom flattened a hand against my back and slowly rubbed firm circles, dulling the pain.

"You should lay down," he mumbled against my hair.

I worried my lip and assessed him. If I did, would he leave? "Will you stay?"

"If you want me here, then there is nowhere else I'd rather be." He scooped me into his arms, pulling a squeak from my lips. "Bed or sofa? I'm fine with either."

"Bed."

He stepped into my room and stopped, taking in the space. When I painted the wall behind my bed a blood red, Avery and Jana had doubted my design skills. But after I'd added the black furniture and white bedding, along with pops of red on the opposite wall and dresser, they had to admit it was killer.

"I expected the room to be overly feminine, I guess, but this fits better. Sexy." Arms tightening around me, he swallowed. "Let's get you as comfortable as we can."

He tucked me into bed, and I snuggled into the mountain of pillows and willed my body to unclench.

He tossed his jacket onto the chair in the corner, but rather than climb in beside me like I expected, he strode out of the room. I blinked at the empty doorway, confused, but before I could make sense of what was going on, he was back with a wrapped package. He set it down next to the bed rather than handing it to me.

"Is that not for me?" I tried not to pout, but I loved a present.

He chuckled. "Who else would it be for?"

"So are you just teasing me with it?" Giving up the battle to remain unaffected, I frowned and set the half-eaten ice cream on my side table.

"Are you up for opening it now? If you want to just lay here and watch TV, I'm good with that." He glanced at the flat-screen on the wall over my dresser and rolled his eyes. "Of course you're watching Neil Caffrey."

"You know how much I love this show. Although." I played with the edge of his cream cashmere quarter-zip. "I think I'm starting to find that a dependable older man is much more sexy."

Growling, he cupped my cheek, his warmth radiating through me, and dropped his lips to mine. Rather than sexual, it felt like peace. Like finally finding the place I belonged.

In the past, a kiss could turn me on or fire me up. But never had it settled my soul and made me think I'd found home.

He pulled back.

"If I give you your gift, will that inspire you to be nice to me?" I teased, planting my hands on the mattress so I could get up.

Gently, he gripped my wrists, holding me in place. "Don't get up. What do you need?"

"There's an envelope on my bar with your name on it."

He pushed to his feet and stalked out of the room. A moment later, he reappeared holding a white envelope with *Daddy Wilson* scrawled across it.

He dropped to the mattress next to me and flipped it between his fingers.

"Open it."

Obediently, he slipped a large finger under the flap and ripped it open. As he pulled out the small stack of papers, his forehead scrunched and his lips parted.

"Is this a contract to buy the Homer?"

I nodded. "I can't afford to buy it for you, but I figured you'd be okay footing the bill for the painting at the top of your wish list. And I got him to agree to sell it for a hundred thousand less than you were willing to pay..."

He blinked at me, his mouth still hanging open.

My stomach flipped and my hands shook. Dammit. I was sure he'd love this. Had I been wrong? "I just thought—"

Before I could finish the thought, he pressed his mouth to mine.

"You're amazing," he mumbled against my lips.

I was breathless when he finally pulled back.

"Pat and Larry have been trying to get this guy to bite for four years." He shook his head. "How?"

I shrugged. "I know the seller. He's like you. He wants works of art to be appreciated, not hidden away. If you approve the contract, you'll be required to display it in a gallery for at least twelve out of every twenty-four months."

"Not an issue." He smiled.

Like every time he graced me with one of those rare smiles, my heart skipped. I should have been terrified of falling so hard for this man, but when he was near, all my fear evaporated.

"Your turn now?" He tipped his head toward the wrapped gift.

I nodded, thankful that he'd come. Normally, I preferred to be left alone in my misery, but all I wanted now was to snuggle and laugh with the man next to me.

He pulled the twelve-by-sixteen-inch package onto the bed. It was wrapped with a precision I'd never achieve but was Tom's signature style.

One tug of the paper, and I caught sight of a canvas covered in what looked like snow.

My breath caught. "No way." The words were barely a mumble as I gently removed the paper. "Oh my god." With a hand clapped to my mouth, I blinked back tears. "*Bridge of Snow.*"

It was as beautiful as I remembered. Every stroke was thick with emotion.

I looked up at him. "You—but—we weren't..." I forced myself to take a breath. "You got this for me?"

How was it possible that I'd become the lucky bitch?

"The moment you told me about it, I knew it should be on your wall. Art should be cherished." He smiled. "This piece deserves to be loved as much as you deserve the opportunity to love it."

"Thank you." I leaned over to kiss him, but before I could make contact, my abdomen spasmed painfully, and I gasped.

With an arm around me, he eased me back into the pillows. "Rest, baby girl. I hate seeing you hurting, especially when I can't do anything to help."

My heart panged at the sincerity in his tone. "You being here helps."

"Then I'll always be here."

I chuckled. "My periods aren't as bad as they used to be, but I still end up in bed for a day most months. As much as I appreciate the sentiment, there's no way you can keep that promise."

"Like hell I can't."

I shook my head. "You do remember you travel with a baseball team, right?"

Jaw locked, he rubbed his thumbs lightly against my lower back.

I sighed in contentment. I could handle any kind of pain as long as he was by my side.

"Can I ask you something?"

I nodded.

"Is the endometriosis the reason you don't want kids?"

I sighed. "That's part of it. It doesn't mean I *can't* have kids." Over the years, doctors had assured me that I had options. "A lot of people do, though it's not always easy and can come with a lot of stress and disappointment along the way." Many people willingly took on that emotional rollercoaster because they wanted children that much. "I've never felt like I needed to have kids of my own to be happy. I can admit that I'm kinda selfish. I like spending money on shoes and going out on a whim and living in a tidy apartment. I want to travel, see the world. I don't want to be tied to one place. Other people's kids are fun, but the best part is knowing I can give them back." I leaned into his shoulder.

His chest moved up and down, but he didn't say anything.

"I'm excited for the day my friends have kids, and I love my nieces. That's enough for me."

He smiled down at me. "It's a good answer. And it's a relief to know that being past the kid raising stage of my life won't affect your dreams. Because I want to give you everything, not take it away."

"You don't need to give me everything, Tom." I swallowed and let him have a scary truth. "But maybe together, we could have everything we ever needed."

He pressed his lips into the top of my head as the bigger words I couldn't say yet hung in the air around us.

As the night went on and we snuggled and watched *White Collar*, it became pretty clear that this had been my best Christmas in a long time. It was terrifying, how right the world felt with Tom at my side, because the moment we went public, it could all go wrong.

Daddy Wilson

25

Baby Girl: What do you normally do for New Year's?

Me: Usually I go to the party at your parents' club or hang out with Leo and the guys.

Baby Girl: And this year?

Me: GIF of a sigh

Me: I had plans, but something came up.

Baby Girl: Oh. Avery invited me to Ground Zero with the team, but I hoped you might man up and invite me to spend the evening with you.

Me: You have a standing invitation to be where I am from now until the end of time.

Baby Girl: GIF of a girl saying awww and clutching her chest.

Me: So if you want to pass on the fun and see what the two of us can come up with, then I'd love to have you come by my place.

Baby Girl: Where you lead, I will follow, babe.

Me: I plan on leading you into the hot tub.

Baby Girl: Happy New Year to me!

Baby Girl: Wait, you're not cooking, right?

Me: Why wouldn't I? I've cooked meals for you for years.

Baby Girl: Yeah, the thing is…you're bad at it.

Me: What?

Baby Girl: I'll bring dinner. Don't worry. You have plenty of other skills we can put to good use. Especially in the hot tub.

Me: You're killing me, baby girl.

Daddy Wilson
26

"CAFFREY, NO."

He looked up with big, sad blue eyes and tipped his head to the side, confused. Probably because he didn't have a clue what I was saying.

"No," I said again, hoping he'd get the point that I didn't want him to eat my shoe. Or pee on the floor or lick me.

How did I end up here?

Squatting, I glared at the dark brown puppy whose tail was thumping against the hardwood floor.

"We don't eat anything but our food." I smacked the back of my hand against my palm, and the eight-week-old chocolate lab barked. "We don't pee inside." I cocked a brow, and he barked again. "And we don't lick people." As if on command, he jumped up and licked my face.

With a hiss, I stood again. I'd brought the puppy home two days ago and had demanded Jess come over and train him. After two sessions, he still peed on the floor and licked me. I couldn't stay mad, though. He was too damn cute.

I scooped him up and headed for the living room. Wren would be walking through the door any minute. She'd been busy with the Christmas auction this week, and I'd been occupied with finding, picking up, and trying to train the damn dog. The chocolate lab was a present for her, and yet I wasn't sure the thorn in my side could really be considered a gift.

When the doorbell chimed, I hollered, "Come in, baby girl." Then I growled at the adorable puppy in my arms. "You be good. We want her to love you."

As the front door opened, I set the puppy down, my gut twisting with nerves. Like I expected, he rushed straight for Wren.

"Oh my gosh!" Before I even got around the sofa and into the foyer, she'd dropped her things onto the floor.

"Aren't you the sweetest thing ever."

I winced at the telltale slurping sound of Caffrey's tongue against skin.

Instead of lurching back, Wren giggled. "Aw, little man. I love you too."

She was sprawled on the floor, surrounded by grocery bags and her duffel, with the puppy jumping all over her. When his paw caught in her black-and-white sweater, I froze, expecting her to freak out.

"Careful, dude, you'll get hurt." She pulled his too-big-for-his-body paw free, not seeming to mind that he'd snagged her sweater.

"I see you met the reason we're staying in tonight."

She peered up at me from beneath her long lashes, eyes sparkling. "Where did you find him?"

"As of two days ago, he's officially part of the Wilson family." I leaned on the doorframe, watching as Caffrey flopped onto his back, legs splayed.

"You hear that, baby?" She rubbed his belly. "You get a Daddy Wilson now too."

I threw my head back and barked a laugh.

"Let's get him." Wren snickered.

The next thing I knew, I was engulfed in perfume and puppy scent as they both kissed my cheeks.

"Enough." I pushed the dog away as I wrapped Wren in my arms and planted my lips firmly on hers.

Caffrey yelped, and she pulled away to let him down. Instantly, he raced out of the room.

"Caffrey, no."

"Caffrey?" She lifted one sculpted brow. I wondered how she'd feel about my naming the little guy after her favorite art thief from *White Collar*.

"I couldn't call him Peter, because we both know the rigid, grumpy FBI agent is pretty much me," I grumbled.

Burying her face in my neck, she stifled a laugh. "It's perfect. I can't believe you got a dog. What were you thinking?"

I inhaled deeply, forcing myself to meet her eye and give her the full truth, no matter how vulnerable it made me feel.

"I never want you to be alone again. You were right the other day when you said that I can't always be there with you. But you told me if I couldn't, I should get a chocolate lab to fill in when I traveled."

As much as I wished I could be there for her at any time, day or night, I had no plans to retire from coaching for a long while.

She sucked in a quick breath.

"He'll be trained soon"—I hoped to God—"and there to snuggle with you when I can't be."

She fell against me, molding into my chest. "No one would believe you're this sweet."

"Because I'm not sweet." I wrapped my arms around her. "And we can't leave him alone for too long because he'll either pee on my shit or eat something that's not food."

She threw her head back, cackling. "I love that you got a dog."

My heart pinched at those words. They almost sounded like what I wanted to hear, and yet they weren't even close.

"You get the damn dog. I'll get the bags." I released her and headed for the shit she'd dropped when she arrived.

As I watched her over the next few hours, I wondered why I bothered to pay a trainer. The woman was a dog whisperer. Before the end of the night, she had Caffrey curled up and sound asleep by the heater on my roof deck after he'd pottied out back in the grass.

"It'll be warm enough for him over there?" Wren asked, eyeing the sitting area where the puppy slept peacefully.

I popped the cork on the champagne and filled two flutes. Midnight was less than half an hour away, and we had Ryan Seacrest playing on my outdoor television so we wouldn't miss the ball drop. Not that either of us seemed to be interested in the fanfare.

"I promise he'll be perfectly content." I pulled my shirt over my head. "That area." I tipped my head toward the covered outdoor living space surrounded by slatted privacy walls. "Is always a balmy seventy. Unlike over here." Shivering, I pulled back the hot tub cover. "Caffrey will be fine. Let's get in before we freeze."

"Fine." She slipped her cover-up over her head, and my heart stopped.

Fuck me. Wren Jacobs in a black lace bikini was perfection. All smooth skin and sleek curves. There wasn't a better view anywhere in the world.

I didn't move. Like a statue frozen with a champagne flute in each hand, I watched as she climbed the steps and slowly slipped into the water, sending the steam rising off it swirling.

Sinking low, she groaned. "I love a hot tub."

That word was driving. me crazy, she loved my dog and she loved my hot tub. But did she love me? I wanted her to love me. I swallowed. Because I loved her.

I blew out a breath, subconsciously I probably already knew this. But I hadn't acknowledged the L word until this moment. I loved my daughter. I loved my job. I had loved my parents, and I'd worked to love my ex-wife. But Avery aside, loving someone or something had never come as easily as it did with Wren. It was like breathing. Like she was made for me to love.

"Are you coming in or are you just going to stand there and look hot as fuck with all the abs and shit?" She hadn't opened her eyes and wasn't looking at me, but her words boosted me anyway.

"Oh, I'm coming in, baby girl." I rushed up the stairs and set the glasses in the cup holders. Then I slid into the steamy water next to her and hoisted her onto my lap, settling her ass against my already hardening cock. Gut tightening at the pressure, I kissed her pulse point. "How do you want to ring in the new year?" I asked into her hair.

"Mmm." She tilted her head, causing my lips to drag along her skin. "I wouldn't mind having you inside me while you moan my name."

"While *I* moan *your* name?"

She peered over her shoulder, her lips quirking mischievously.

I cocked a brow. "I think you have that backward." I ghosted my hands up the soft skin of her stomach until I reached the underside of her breasts.

She rolled her hips once. "Prove it."

"Oh, I'd love to." Beneath the triangles of her bikini top, I found her nipples peaked. The wet material rubbed against the back of my hands as I pinched the tight buds. While I toyed with her, I peppered her neck with kisses, pausing below her ear, in the spot that made her squirm, and lapped at the hollow with my tongue.

Her chest rose and fell against my hands as her breathing quickened. She shifted on my lap, rubbing her ass against my aching cock.

Biting back a groan, I caressed her abdomen, teasing her until I found the top edge of her swimsuit bottoms.

She arched against me and rocked up, whimpering.

"What do you need?" I whispered against her ear.

A shiver worked its way through her. "You. I need you to touch me, Daddy Wilson."

Fuck. Those words were fire in my veins. Without hesitation, I slipped my hand under the fabric and between her thighs. And when I slid my fingers through her lips, her breathing hitched. The second I dipped a finger inside her, she rocked against my palm.

"You like that, don't you?" My words barely a rumble against her ear. "My finger claiming your pussy while you use my hand to get off?"

She dropped her head back against my shoulder and offered her lips to me. Tongue thrusting against hers, I swallowed her moan, dominating her mouth and her pussy. Claiming both. My cock was hard as stone throbbing, but it wasn't the only ache. A powerful emotion tugged inside my chest, making me feel unsteady.

She writhed against my palm, swirling her hips, chasing her pleasure. Each panting breath that left her lips settled deep inside me, as if she was worming her way into a place no one had ever found. And maybe she was.

With a thumb, I flicked her clit, then followed the move with a curl of my finger, hitting the spot that never failed to make her scream. Fuck, I needed her to come like this, then she could come on my cock.

"Right there." She rocked hard, her head thrashing back and forth, her pussy quivering. I bit down on her shoulder, and in return, her core tensed, gripping my fingers tight and pulsing. "*Yes.*" The word left her in a long, low moan.

"You're so fucking beautiful when you come. I could watch you do this all day, baby girl." I toyed with her until her orgasm ebbed, making sure each wave of pleasure rocked her to the core. When her body relaxed, she slumped against me, panting.

Standing, I spun us both. "Bend over. Hands on the edge," I ordered. "You're going to do that again, but this time on my cock."

The second she was steady, I tugged her suit bottoms down her legs.

"Spread." Heart hammering, I yanked off my own suit, releasing my cock, already leaking, begging for the woman before me.

I guided my dick over her pussy, pulling another moan from her. Over and over, I teased us both. My hands were shaking with the need to slip inside her, but I willed my body to hold back, to be patient.

"Either put your cock inside me, or I'll do it for you," Wren threatened.

The chuckle that escaped me was pure gravel. "There's my needy girl." Instead of giving her what she demanded, I gave her a good hard swat on the ass. Her already warm skin reddened in response. My abs tightened and my cock throbbed at the sight of my mark on her.

Mark her, claim her, own her. My body vibrated with the desperate need for all of it. I swatted again.

"Fuck, I love that." She groaned. "Do it again, but this time with your cock in my pussy, Daddy Wilson."

My threadbare restraint disappeared. I notched myself to her and plunged into her wet cunt, bottoming out.

Fuck. She was heaven. Water splashed around us as I thrust. The way her pussy gripped my cock as I spanked her ass had my knees almost buckling.

"God, yes. More." She rutted back against me, her breath leaving her in a burst every time I drove into her. Hitting the spot that made her legs shake. "Yes, right there." She whimpered. "Faster."

What she wanted, I'd give her.

Hips pumping, I slapped her ass once more, then soothed the sting. "Come on, baby girl. Come for me."

The words had hardly left my lips when she shattered around me. I locked my knees to keep them from buckling under me. While she moaned my name, pleasure erupted through me, fierce and all-consuming. I let myself fall under the spell, under her spell.

"Fuck." I slammed into her again and again as waves of pleasure racked my body. I only slowed when we were both wrung out, curling over her as she leaned on the edge of the tub.

Those three little words were on the tip of my tongue as I pressed my lips to her shoulder. But she shivered in the cool air, so I pulled back, bringing her with me.

I sat on the bench, guiding her onto my lap into the warm water. For one breath, she reclined against my chest. Then she spun and settled her thighs on either side of mine. Pride rose in my chest as I took her in. Her cheeks were flushed, her dark eyes deep pools of contentment, and a ghost of a smile pulled at her lips. She was gorgeous, she was happy, she was mine.

She raked her hands through my hair, pulling a groan from deep in my chest. Our faces were just inches apart. Every exhale from her lips brushed mine.

Behind us, the countdown had begun.

"Four, three, two, one," she whispered along with it.

"Happy New Year," we said in unison. In the next heartbeat, I dropped my lips to hers.

Maybe it was only a simple holiday, but it felt like the start of something more. Like the start of forever.

The only sour note was how long I'd have to wait to tell the world that Wren was mine, since my daughter's wedding was weeks away.

I might have planned a life that revolved around order, but that was long gone. Because now that I had this woman in my arms, I'd never let her go.

Wren
27

Daddy Wilson: I think Caffrey needs you to come over tonight.

Me: You said that yesterday.

Daddy Wilson: I am not above using your love for my dog as an excuse to get to see my girl.

Me: At this rate I might as well be living there. I haven't spent a night at home in over a week.

Daddy Wilson: I am not opposed to the idea. And we both know Caffrey would love it.

Me: We have to tell people before we can even joke about that.

Daddy Wilson: In a few weeks, that won't be an issue anymore.

Me: And here I was thinking that in a few weeks, it's going to be a major issue.

Me: I know, I know, you're rolling your eyes at me.

Daddy Wilson: You know me so well. And since you haven't said no, I'll order dinner.

Me: Yes, please. Don't cook.

Daddy Wilson: You never used to give me so much shit about my cooking.

Me: Because back then, eating at your place was one of only a few ways I could see you. Now I get to do that without choking down bad food.

Daddy Wilson: Don't sass me, baby girl.

Me: What if I like the punishment?

Daddy Wilson: You're going to kill me.

Daddy Wilson
28

I SCANNED THE CROWDED ROOM. The co-ed shower was going better than I'd thought it would when Avery told me about the idea. I expected it to be nothing but presents and stupid "don't say bride" games that no one wanted to play. I hadn't factored in that Wren was planning it. She created a casino night, and all the money the house won went to Chris and Avery as a wedding gift. They were donating it all to Blondie's Birds, the charity Chris had started for the Boston Zoo's birds.

Chris and Avery already lived together, and since they didn't need things for their place, gifts were adventures for their two-week honeymoon. Dinners at restaurants she'd picked out, honeymoon suites, and couples' massages. My girl was creative, and not a single present had to be opened.

It had been entertaining. I'd played a few rounds of blackjack and some craps while trying not to watch my girl flit around the room in that gold dress, making sure everything was organized.

Not one moment was boring. Sure, it was a bit torturous watching her and not being allowed to touch her. But she was coming back to my place after she was done here, and I'd have the entire night to enjoy her. And my daughter was happy and full of smiles. So I had nothing to complain about.

As the night began to wind down and there were only about twenty of us left, I sought out my ex-wife, Kristine, and her husband, Dave, who were sitting at side-by-side slot machines.

"Got a minute?" I asked when I sidled up next to Kristine.

Her long blond hair tipped over her shoulder as she looked up at me. "For you, I've got exactly five minutes," she teased. Beside her, Dave chuckled.

"Need a refill?" I asked, pointing to his beer. "It's almost last call."

He lifted his chin. "Thanks. I'll make sure no one steals your win, babe."

Kristine smiled. "Aw, my hero." She stood and wandered toward the bar with me. "What's up?"

"I've been seeing someone." I cleared my throat. "And it's serious."

"That's..." She gave me a small smile, though her brow creased in question. "Great."

Twenty-some years ago, when she and I had this conversation in reverse, it had made more sense. We had a five-year-old, and bringing Dave into Avery's life was going to affect her. Although Kristine hadn't been the most consistent parent in the world, she loved Avery and the two of us co-parented well. But now Avery was twenty-nine, so my ex-wife was probably wondering why the fuck I was talking to her about this. But Avery's initial reaction might be hurt or upset, and I wanted her to have someone to talk with about it. Someone who already knew and had already had time to process it.

"I'm worried about how Avery is going to take it, so I was hoping for some support."

At the bar, I ordered refills for both her and Dave.

"Why would she care?" she asked, frowning. "It's not like you're dating her best friend."

Eyes pinched shut, I sighed. Maybe Wren and I hadn't hidden our attraction as well as I'd thought if everyone was so quick to guess.

"Oh shit. Wren?" Kristine's voice was high-pitched.

I opened my eyes and held up a hand. "Shh. Kris. Literally no one but Leo knows."

"You should probably be more worried about telling Heath than telling Avery." Despite her words, the smile pulling at her lips told me my ex was happy for me.

"Thanks for that." I frowned.

She shook her head and glanced past me. I followed her gaze, finding Wren watching us carefully. Her shoulders were pulled back tight with nerves. She knew I was talking to Kristine about this today. I didn't want to do it at the wedding, and as soon as Avery found out about us, she would call her mother. Wren wasn't jealous of my ex-wife, but she worried about her best friend's mother's reaction.

"Can you do me a favor?" I muttered.

"Besides talk Avery off a ledge when she finds out?" My ex chuckled.

"Yes, besides that."

"What?" She peered up at me.

But I couldn't pull my eyes off the woman across the room who was shifting on her feet and worrying her bottom lip.

"Can you send the signal women put off that says *hey, I'm cool with you being with my ex* Wren's way?"

With a laugh, she blew a kiss to Wren, then gave her a finger wave.

Immediately, the tension eased out of my girl's body.

"It's cute how gone you are for her, but I'd stop staring like that if you don't want people to know."

Fuck. She was right. I forced my gaze back to the bar, where the bartender had set the drinks, and tossed a twenty into the tip jar.

"You two look cozy." Leo appeared next to Kristine and wrapped an arm around her shoulder.

"He was just telling me about his new girlfriend."

"Oh, fun. Now I'll have company to watch the train wreck with." He chuckled.

"I'm not telling anyone else tonight," I grumbled.

Leo knew the plan and he was on board with waiting until after the wedding.

"In the end, Avery will be okay with it." My ex-wife patted my arm.

"It's Heath who's going to kill the bastard," Leo added.

She shrugged. "I agree. What do you think? Will he toss Tom off his sailboat or bury him on the golf course?"

"Golf course." Leo tapped the neck of his beer bottle against her wineglass.

I scowled at both of them. "I'll leave you to plot my funeral."

By now, the only people left were our closest friends and family. Even most of the team had gone home. From what I could tell, only Emerson, my third baseman—as well as Chris's best friend and soon-to-be brother-in-law—was still here.

So I headed toward the Jacobses table and dropped back into the seat where I'd spent most of my night.

"Everything okay with Kris?" Heath glanced over at her.

I didn't follow his gaze. She and Leo were probably still laughing about my death.

"Yeah, she's excited about the wedding. I've done my best to stay out of the way unless I'm presented with a bill to pay."

"I remember those days with Lottie."

Their older daughter had been married for several years and had already given Heath and Colleen two grandkids.

"We might be doing it again soon." Colleen tried to hide her smirk behind her glass.

Heath sighed. "I keep telling you not to get your hopes up."

"And I keep telling you that our daughter is dating someone. I'm sure of it. She only calls me from work, and twice now, when I tried to come by to see her, she's given me the lamest excuses about why I couldn't."

I locked my jaw. One of those calls wasn't from work, and I'd heard the lame excuse.

"Two days ago, she tried to convince me that she'd waxed her floor and it couldn't be walked on until morning, so she was stuck in bed."

Heath scoffed. "I bought that apartment five years ago, and that girl has never waxed her floors."

That excuse was worse than the one about the facial I'd heard.

Wren was not the type of woman who scrubbed or waxed floors. A chuckle escaped me, but I quickly turned it into a cough.

"See?" Colleen pointed at me. "He believes me."

I schooled my features and held both hands up. "Don't drag me into your relationship."

Heath draped an arm over his wife's shoulders. "I know you want her to settle down with one of the men you keep shoving her way and give you grandkids, but don't give yourself false hope."

It was hard to fight a wince, because although I could promise to take care of their daughter, giving them grandkids was off the table. And the idea that Colleen was trying to set Wren up on dates had my hands balling into fists.

I forced myself to take a calming breath. "She does seem happy lately." I couldn't help but throw that out there. I was hoping like hell they'd noticed her contentment.

"She does," Colleen said.

Heath narrowed his eyes. "When have you seen her?"

I shrugged, trying to play it off. "I've stopped in to talk to Erin at the auction house a few times recently. Plus she's been helping me purchase some pieces, so we've crossed paths."

Head tilted, he examined me, his mind working. "Wait…"

Dread sank in my gut like a lead ball. Maybe I'd pushed too far by saying she was happy. I wasn't sure how to walk it back.

"What, hun?" In what felt like slow-motion, Colleen reached over and patted his arm.

Angling closer, he lowered his head. "You and Erin?" His eyes cut over to Leo, who had dated her for six years, before he peered over at Erin two tables away.

My entire body relaxed, and a laugh bubbled out of me. "No." I shook my head. "Definitely no. Never." His suspicious gaze didn't leave me, but I held both hands up. "I swear."

He shook his head. "I don't get why you're being so damn secretive about the woman, then. Why not bring her tonight?"

I shrugged. "It's Avery's week. The last thing I want to do is take attention away from her."

"What are you all whispering about?"

I nearly jumped at the sound of Wren's voice so close. I tried not to smile at her but failed. In her gold dress, she was glowing, and her red lips had been taunting me all night.

"Just saying what a great job you did putting this together, darling. You're a natural at event planning."

Wren shifted away from her mother and stood on my far side, her eyes blazing. "I'm not marrying a senator and putting on charity events forever, Mom. Get that idea out of your head."

Don't react. Don't react. Fuck, the idea of her marrying anyone but me made my skin crawl. I didn't want to hear about it, think about it, picture it. Yet for the second time in fifteen minutes, I was forced to.

"Don't be dramatic. It doesn't have to be a senator." Heath sat back in his chair and crossed his arms. "But it wouldn't hurt to find someone."

I hadn't realized they had such an obsession with setting their daughter up with a man. What the fuck? I would have preferred Avery not date at all before she met Chris. Focus on her friends, her schooling, her career—that's what I always told her.

At the frustration locking Wren's tight jaw, I was pretty sure my way of handling Avery was better than whatever this was.

"The real point is you did an amazing job," I rushed out. "We're all impressed."

Onyx eyes softening, she shifted her attention from her mother to me. "Thanks." She surveyed the room. "With all the gifts, they'll definitely have the sexiest honeymoon ever."

I groaned. "Please don't go there."

"Married people have sex. Loosen up, Daddy Wilson," she taunted, resting a hand on my shoulder.

Through my white button-down, I could feel the heat of her palm as she squeezed.

"Stop annoying Tom," Heath muttered, picking up his drink.

"Fine, fine." I didn't have to look at her to know she was rolling her eyes. "I'm going to do one more round to make sure the staff has everything handled."

"Don't work too hard, baby girl."

Next to me, Heath coughed and slammed his glass onto the table so hard I was surprised it didn't shatter. "Son of a bitch."

In that moment, all the air was sucked from my lungs, and my heart fell through the floor.

Oh shit.

What had I just done?

Wren
29

WITH MY HEART hammering in my chest, I dropped my hand from Tom's shoulder.

"Tell me I'm imagining this, Tom," my dad snapped, addressing one of his best friends. Steam might have been coming out of his ears for as red as my father's face was. "Tell me right now the woman you've been dating is not my daughter."

There was no way my parents would be reasonable about this. I had always known that. I shouldn't have touched his shoulder, and I shouldn't have teased him while they were right there. I wasn't thinking, and now…

"Tom?" my father gritted out. Luckily, the party had mostly dispersed. But Emerson, Chris's best friend, and his fiancée, Gianna, moved closer. As did Avery's mother and stepdad and Leo.

I frantically looked for Avery, but I didn't see her.

Jana was across the room, and when she met my eye, she mouthed, "What the fuck?"

Looking away, I swallowed, fighting back the panic bubbling inside me. I wasn't sure what Tom would do. If he didn't lie, this was going to explode.

Tom pushed to his feet and shot me an apologetic look.

Dammit, he was going to deny it. My shoulders slumped in disappointment. But instead of telling my father he was wrong, he took my hand firmly in his and lifted his chin.

"I can't tell you that, Heath."

My stomach flipped. How the hell was it possible to be both thrilled and terrified in the same second? Despite how impossible it seemed, that was exactly how I felt. Tom Wilson was willing to blow up his life to claim me in front of every person who mattered to him.

His fingers tightened, grounding me, reminding me that we were in this together.

"No." My dad slapped the white tablecloth with all his might, causing the dishes to rattle and knocking over my mother's wineglass. But no one moved. Every person in the room was frozen. "You are not dating my daughter."

"Who?" Avery stepped up to the table, brow furrowed. Her long blond waves brushed over her shoulder as she looked from my dad to hers and then to where my hand was locked in Tom's.

Tom's body tightened next to me. "I'm sorry, Avy." His throat worked as he swallowed, and my heart clenched with sorrow for him. "I really wanted to talk to you about this first."

So had I. We should have. The guilt that we hadn't clawed up my throat. This time I was the one giving a reassuring squeeze.

He spun back to my dad. "I have been dating Wren. I won't pretend that's not true. She's who I've been talking about for over a month now."

Avery pulled in a sharp breath just as my father lunged for Tom. Leo launched himself across two chairs to force my father back into his seat. As people gasped and jumped out of the way, Chris tucked Avery into his side and glared at us. Fuck. We were ruining her party. At this point, though, I wasn't sure how to stop any of it.

"What the hell, Leo?" My father shifted, pushing his friend away.

"You can't hit him, Heath. He's your best friend." Leo shook his head.

My father's voice rose, loud enough to be heard over the murmurs and not so quiet comments from the group that had gathered. "He's sleeping with my daughter."

"I'm in love with your daughter," Tom said, his voice even louder.

Once again, everyone froze.

All the air in my lungs escaped in one firm whoosh. Jaw unhinged and wide-eyed, I stared at him. He spun and cupped my cheek. "You should have heard those words first, but I know you know it. You feel it. I love you, and we'll get through this."

I nodded. He loved me.

He pressed his lips to my forehead, and all the tension eased out of my body.

"I love you too." It was barely a whisper, but his small smile told me he'd heard it.

"No," my father repeated. "I'm not allowing this."

My vision went red around the edges. I was no longer sixteen and his to control. I stepped around Tom. "I'm an adult and you don't get a vote, Dad."

"Oh, really?" He cocked a brow. "An adult? You live in an apartment I bought and you drive a car I paid for. Hell, I even bought your phone."

None of that was a lie, but he was acting as if I was always after him for a handout, when I could support myself just fine. "My apartment was my graduation gift," I fired back. "You gave me the car for my birthday several years ago. The car that I pay to maintain and insure. My phone was a Christmas present last year. But if I'd known those gifts were your way of controlling my life, I wouldn't have taken them." I stalked to my table and swiped my purse off the surface. "Now that I know—" One at a time, I dropped the key fob to my apartment, my car key, and my phone onto the tablecloth in front of him.

He blinked up at me, his face a mask of betrayal and disappointment.

"Oh. I almost forgot that Mom gave me this purse for my birthday. And I'm pretty sure this watch came from you guys too." I slipped the gold band from my wrist and dropped it onto the pile, then tossed my purse too. "We good now?" I didn't even wait for a response before I spun and eyed my best friend.

Jaw tense, she averted her gaze. Shit.

"Avery." Swallowing past the boulder in my throat, I moved her way.

Before I could get to her, Chris pulled her closer and shook his head.

I was stunned, staring at them, when Jana stepped in front of me. "Why don't you go? I'll clean up here, and then we'll talk. Now's not the time." Very deliberately, she panned the room, reminding me we had an audience.

My stomach dropped. Fuck. She was right.

Avery was flanked by Chris and her mother. None of whom would look at me. My mother and Leo were talking to my father. Everyone else stared at me. Including Erin.

Fuck.

My heart skipped. I hadn't realized she was still here.

It wasn't only Tom who'd blown up his life today. Apparently I had too.

With a nod at Jana, I strode out of the room. It wasn't until I was out the door that it hit me: I didn't have a car or a phone to call an Uber. Hell, I didn't even have a home anymore.

Eyes burning, I blinked back tears. For a moment, I thought my legs might give out, but before I could fall, a set of strong arms embraced me from behind. I spun around and let Tom pull me into his chest.

"That was a disaster." A single tear crested my lashes before I could stop it. "The exact type of chaos you hate." I shook my head. "Maybe we're not good for each other."

"No." He tightened his hold on me. "I hate chaos, but I was the cause of that clusterfuck. I should have talked to your dad before now." Lips pressed to the crown of my head, he inhaled deeply. "And you're wrong about that last part. You're one of the best things that has ever happened to me. I might not be good for most people, but baby girl, I'm good for you. I'll take care of every obstacle in our way to prove it."

His every word was fierce, determined. I snuggled deeper into his chest. Everything was a mess right now. And yet I felt safe, protected, and cared for more than I ever had before.

"Let's go home, baby girl."

Home. The strangest part about tonight was that I already felt like I was home.

Daddy Wilson
30

Me: Can we talk?

Avy: We have to. I realize that. But I'm not ready yet. So I'm not throwing a temper tantrum. I'm just saying give me some time okay Dad?

Me: As long as you need Avy. I love you.

Me: I know you're mad, but man, you're one of my best friends. Can we at least have a conversation?

Heath: Is she staying with you?

Me: Yes.

Me: Heath, it's been three hours. Come on.

Leo: You're still alive, right?

Me: You're not funny

Leo: You doing okay?

Me: I'm more worried about her than I am about myself.

Leo: Yeah, because you love her.

Me: So fucking much.

Leo: The good news is I no longer have competition for the title of your best man.

Me: I hate you.

Leo: I hope you laughed.

Chris: Since we weren't planning a rehearsal dinner, Avery and I are just going to do a walk-through of the wedding with Puff on Friday. No one else is invited.

Me: Okay.

Chris: It's not completely because she doesn't want to see you. It will be better for Puff too.

Me: Sure

Avy: Could you come a little later than we originally planned on Saturday? I think it'll be better if it's just Mom until an hour or so before the wedding.

Me: Sure, Avy. Whatever you want.

Wren
31

BY MONDAY, I still hadn't bothered to get a new phone, which meant I was paying for a phone plan I wasn't using. Tom offered to take me to pick up a new one. Instead, I'd snuggled with him and Caffrey on the sofa, unwilling to step outside my little bubble of peace. This morning, though, I was fully out of the bubble and back at work, which meant I needed a phone. And I needed a place to live.

I'd had the doorman let me in my apartment to grab some things this weekend, and Tom didn't mind that I was staying with him. I'd been staying there every night anyway.

But I was furious. My parents' love shouldn't have come with strings. And discovering that it did had shaken me. Maybe I had over-reacted. I didn't know. But I was devastated.

At the sound of a knock on my door, I looked up, and when I discovered Erin standing at the threshold, I fought back a wince.

I licked my lips and garnered what little strength I'd held on to over the past couple of days. "Hi."

"Can I come in?" she asked, crossing her arms over her chest.

I nodded.

Her expression remained neutral as she settled into the chair across from me. "Want to talk about anything?"

I might not want to talk, but I needed to say a few things. "I feel like I should probably apologize."

Her eyes narrowed and her brow crinkled in confusion. "For?"

"You warned me to be professional before I went to New York, and I failed you."

"Ah." Nodding, she folded her hands in her lap. "Do you feel like Tom Wilson got less than stellar service working with you?"

That gave me pause. "No. Of course not." I might have crossed lines, but I'd done a damn good job acquiring that piece.

"I haven't heard anything to counter that either." She frowned. "Obviously, your involvement with Tom means I shouldn't ask for his opinion, but Kline said you handled Tom's piss-poor attitude without missing a beat. He said you didn't panic when Tom locked himself out of the room and you remained discreet about your travels and the art throughout the trip."

That was all true.

"The staff at the MET raved about you. Your skill, your attention to detail, your professionalism. You reported in the night before with a storm update plan and adjusted flights when you needed to. Then you made it home and ran an auction the next day without missing a beat. All of that for a trip that was forced on you last minute with a client you had never worked with."

My heart fluttered, but I wasn't sure whether it was in appreciation or dread.

"I've been telling Tom for a good two years that the two of you were perfect for each other."

Shock hit me like an electric current. What? I assumed that, from the outside, most people would see us as completely incompatible. Maybe because that's what I'd thought for years. Even Tom didn't see it as easily as Erin apparently had.

"I'm not upset that you're dating." She sighed. "I'm a bit bummed that you won't be working for me forever, but working together in a different capacity will be fun."

I pursed my lips. "What?"

"You'll have the job you've always wanted when you work for

Tom. I'd love to help you facilitate his art purchases and come to your events as a colleague and a friend." She smiled. "But you won't be here much longer because you're going to curate and run what will become one of the biggest galleries in Boston."

Spurred on by a wave of pride, I sat a bit straighter in my seat. "You really have that much faith in me?"

"I'm good at spotting talent, Wren. And I saw it in you years ago." She reached across the desk and patted my hand.

"Thanks."

"So," she said, pulling back. "I'm not offering you Pat's job."

I frowned. It was disappointing, but even if she had offered it, I couldn't have taken it. Not if Tom really wanted to open a gallery in the next two years. "I assumed."

"But it's only because you have a foot in the door of a bigger adventure. It's an opportunity I want you to take."

I nodded.

"And Wren." She stood, smoothing her skirt. "The rest will get easier, I promise. He's worth the headache."

I couldn't help but give her a small smile. "That, I'm sure of."

But five days later, nothing had gotten easier.

Growing up, Avery had always wanted to get married at my parents' country club, and that was exactly what she and Chris were doing today.

"You sure you're okay?" I asked Tom.

When Avery had asked him not to come to the bridal suite early, he played it off as no big deal, but the way he had shut his eyes and taken a deep breath had my heart cracking in half for the dad that had spent years being there for his daughter.

He squeezed my hand, then gripped the steering wheel again. "Chris texted yesterday and invited me to have lunch with him, his dad, and Emerson at the clubhouse. It's easier for everyone if I'm not there while you're all getting ready. It should have been this way from the start."

That might have been true. He probably would have spent most of the time alone out in the hallway while we were changing. But he and Avery were so close. It was hard to imagine her not wanting him there for every moment today. And as hard as he was trying, the hurt echoed in his eyes.

"I promise I'm good, baby girl."

I needed to get out of the car, but the club that had been like a home away from home my whole life suddenly looked scary and uninviting. Especially since I wasn't sure I'd be welcome. I'd gotten a phone on Monday afternoon and had immediately texted Avery, but she hadn't wanted to talk.

Taking a steadying breath, I dropped Tom's hand and pushed the door open.

He gave me a soft, sad smile. "I'll see you in there."

"I'll be the one in red," I joked as I grabbed my dress and bag out of the back.

As he pulled away, I headed up the path surrounded by piles of January snow. I hadn't even gotten to the door before Jana appeared.

"Ready to talk?" she asked, her red hair blowing in the cold Boston wind.

My throat tightened, making it hard to breathe. I hadn't answered her texts. But besides Avery's, I hadn't answered anyone's. "Sure."

"I only have one thing to say, then the floor is yours." She folded her arms over the red robe embroidered with the word bridesmaid. "You could have told me. I would have squealed in excitement with you. You've had a thing for Mr. Wilson forever. This wouldn't have shocked me. I would have been there for you and helped you tell Avery." She frowned. "I hate that you felt like you couldn't come to me."

"I'm sorry." I sighed. I hadn't worked to keep it from Jana. "It all happened quickly, and now, with everyone upset, it feels weird to say that I'm happy."

She gently took my garment bag, then wrapped her free arm around me. "I think it's amazing. You should have seen the way he glared at everyone as you left the other night. That man is head over heels for you, Wren."

"It's pretty mutual." And it felt nice to admit that without judgment.

She giggled. "I never thought I'd see the day you fell for someone."

"Me either, but I don't want to wreck today with any drama."

She nodded.

Another wind gust ripped around us, and I shivered. "Can we go in, it's freezing." Together we stepped into the club, and Jana led me down to the bridal suite. The closer we got, the faster my heart beat. I wasn't exactly sure how I would be greeted.

Luckily the room wasn't crowded. Kristine and Chris's sister, Gianna, were the only people in the room with Avery.

"Look who I found hanging around," Jana announced.

Avery turned my way while a hairdresser worked on making her straight blond hair fall in beachy waves. She was always gorgeous, but today, she was going to be stunning.

I'd been there months ago when she picked out her dress. We'd laughed about the way Chris's eyes were going to bug out of his head when he saw her. Back then, I thought this day would be filled with nothing but joy. How could it not, when my best friend was finally getting her fairy-tale wedding?

Now, I felt like a different person. My feet felt heavy and I slowed to a stop just inside the door.

Her blue eyes met mine, and she blinked twice. She hadn't told me not to come today, but the blank stare she sent my way wasn't exactly welcoming. With a thick swallow, I considered offering to leave.

Before I could work up the nerve, she waved me over. I moved without hesitation, and as I approached, Kristine and Gianna moved to the far side of the room, giving us a minute.

"Hi." I gave her a small, awkward smile.

"Hi." She sighed and picked at a piece of fuzz on her white satin robe. "I don't want things to be weird today."

"Me either." It killed me to know that I'd made anything about her wedding imperfect.

She met my eye again. "Let's just pretend you didn't hook up with Dad. Then we can move on like it didn't happen."

My stomach dropped as those words ripped through my chest like a knife. Not only was she uninterested in talking things out, but she was writing my relationship with Tom off completely, like it was only a fling.

"You'll be on to someone new by the time I'm home from my trip anyway." With that, she spun back to the mirror.

I was at a loss for words. Was that what she thought of me? That I moved on without a thought? Maybe it was fair; in the past, hadn't I done just that? But back then, I'd never experienced a connection like I had with Tom.

I blinked hard. It hurt that she couldn't see the difference. Not that I'd given her a chance to. And that was on me. I could call her out, but this was her wedding day. I wouldn't make things harder.

"It's your day." The words left my lips almost flatly, and I moved to the far side of the room.

"You okay?" Jana asked

I nodded.

She pursed her lips, her eyes swimming with questions. Thankfully, before she could hound me, the makeup crew walked in and the wedding fun started.

With a glass of champagne in my hand, I plastered on a smile and did my best to stay out of the way. It was nothing like how I'd pictured this day, and this was not me. But I wouldn't cause waves.

After a while, Emerson knocked on the doorframe and sauntered in, tripping on his own feet as he did.

"No men allowed," Gianna, his fiancée, teased.

"No grooms allowed. But men bearing gifts for the bride and the maid of honor should be welcomed with kisses." Holding two envelopes, each with a small box, he bent down to kiss her, but Gianna gave him her cheek.

"Makeup, Em," she chided.

"Makeup is a worse cock-block than my mother," he grumbled, turning to Avery. "From your father, who absolutely adores you and can't wait to see you." He handed her a white envelope and a small box. Then he turned to me and held out the small gold envelope and box. "From the man who apparently adores you too."

My hands shook as I reached for the package. All eyes were on me, Avery's gaze the most palpable. "I didn't know…" What a dumb thing to say. Of course I didn't know he'd have a gift delivered to me. I shook my head.

"Open it, Avy," Kristine prompted, blessedly shifting the attention of the group back to the bride. Where it should be.

I knew what was in the box for Avery, since I'd helped her dad pick it out two weeks ago. A diamond and sapphire tennis bracelet. In all honesty, he didn't need my help. He knew her, and he'd picked the perfect something blue. She turned her back to me, excluding me from the moment.

Respecting her need for space, I stepped away and opened the envelope.

For the first of many big occasions in our life together.

A small something that I hope will always remind you of how grateful I am to have you next to me through all the important days and even the ordinary ones.

Daddy Wilson

My lips tugged up at the corners as I studied the signature. It was the first time he'd ever called himself that. He'd done it on purpose. To make me smile because he knew how hard today would be.

Across the room, Jana and Gianna gasped over the jewelry. Instead of being drawn into the excitement, I couldn't help but worry that if I joined in, I would be an interruption. The idea made my chest hurt. No part of me wanted to be an interruption on my best friend's day. But her comments rang in my ears. She wanted to pretend it hadn't happened. As much as I didn't want to hurt her, to ruin her day, I couldn't deny my connection with Tom.

With a steadying breath, I turned back to the small jewelry box in my hand.

I cracked the gold lid, and my jaw dropped when I caught sight of the heirloom teardrop ruby nestled below a diamond on a rose gold chain. Not only was this perfect to my taste, but it was the perfect complement to my dress. That made sense, since Tom Wilson was a details man. My details man. Heart pounding, I looked up, finding that Avery was watching me, wearing a frown.

The look was a punch to the stomach. I had never wanted my relationship with Tom to cost me my best friend.

Daddy Wilson
32

Baby Girl: You always manage to be perfect, especially when I don't expect it. Today didn't need to be about me.

Me: For me, every day will be about you.

Baby Girl: Again with the too sweet.

Me: How's it going?

Baby Girl: Avery seems happy.

I STARED AT THE MESSAGE, annoyed. As much as I wanted my daughter to be happy today, it shouldn't be at the expense of the woman I loved. Dammit. I shouldn't have had to dance such a fine line. I wanted them both to be happy.

The idea of walking away from Wren was inconceivable, and yet I didn't want to trade my relationship with my daughter. Worse, I didn't want to ruin the girls' relationship, and I had. Making them both unhappy was a knife in my chest.

I understood why Avery was upset. In my ideal world, I would have talked to her first. When it didn't work out that way, I should have forced her to talk to me. But I hadn't wanted to push. Now I was questioning myself and messing things up with Wren. It felt like I was losing the two most important people in my life, and I didn't know how to fix it.

Lunch had been easy. Chris was on cloud nine, without even a hint of any cold feet. I hadn't expected any issues, but it was a comfort to know my daughter was in good hands.

Pacing outside the bridal suite, I checked my watch, then finally knocked on the door.

Jana answered, her eyes bright and her smile wide. "Hey, Mr. Wilson," she chirped. "Welcome to the party." She tilted her head, and her red curls brushed her bare shoulders.

"Everyone decent?" I asked.

"Yeah, Dave's been in here for a while."

"Perfect." I forced a smile and stepped inside. I never let myself get jealous of Avery's stepfather, and I wouldn't start now.

"You look beautiful Avy." I swallowed. All grown up and ready to start her new life.

"Thanks." She beamed and then held out her hand to me. "You got the perfect something blue."

I smiled. "It seemed like you."

"And it matches the earrings Chris got me." She tucked her hair over her shoulder.

"He has good taste." I assured her. "And not just in jewelry."

She rolled her blue eyes.

"I just want to say I'm sorry." I stepped closer.

"No." She shook her head. "We're going to pretend like none of it happened. Just move on."

That was a hard statement to swallow. I was willing to give her the happy wedding day. I wanted it for her. But I couldn't pretend Wren and I had never happened.

Avery turned back to her mother, and my attention got snagged on a head of dark hair in the corner.

Wren.

My heart clenched painfully at the sight. She was stunning, with her dark hair curled and wearing a red dress that matched her lipstick. My breaths came quicker as my entire focus shifted to my girl. Despite how gorgeous she was, it hurt to look at her like this, with hunched shoulders and dull eyes.

"You take my breath away, baby girl."

A smile lifted her lips, and she gave me a thorough once-over. "You don't look so bad yourself."

Chest swelling, I squatted in front of her. "I think it's the red tie. It'd make anyone look good."

"No." She reached up and straightened it, then rested her palms on my chest. "It's not the tie. It's the man wearing it." The soft words settled deep in my bones.

"We need to get pictures with the father of the bride," the photographer called.

"You better go." She brushed a lock of hair off my forehead.

Startled by the flash of a camera nearby, I studied her. "You're not coming?"

She shook her head.

"You're in the wedding party too."

She sighed. "Avery's not happy about us. And although I should." She reached out and linked our hands together. "I can't care enough to walk away from you. But I can care enough to give her space. Especially today. It's her day, and its better if I stay out of the way."

She blinked hard. I turned over my shoulder to see Avery frowning at us.

"Wren."

Expression going stormy, she shook her head. "I might never have dreamed of a wedding, but Avery always has. Today is her day. I won't do anything else to mess it up."

Anger and hurt made my muscles tense. Wren was being a good friend. The problem was that my daughter wasn't.

With a light tap over my heart, she said, "Go be her dad. I'm fine."

Resigned, I pushed to my feet and strode across the room. I obediently posed for pictures, but all the while, my eyes drifted to Wren, who didn't move from the corner. Years from now, Avery would regret that her pre-wedding pictures didn't include her best friend.

Kristine met my eye and gave me a small, helpless shrug. She'd texted me earlier saying Avery didn't even want to talk to her about it.

I'd promised Wren I'd get everyone on board with our relationship, and so far, I'd failed.

I understood Wren not wanting to upset Avery. I wanted my daughter to be happy, to have a wedding day that was magical. But excluding her best friend wasn't the answer. And I hated seeing both of my girls upset.

By the time we lined up to walk down the aisle, the air was uncomfortable with the weight of all the unspoken words hanging between us, and it was clear that ignoring the issue wasn't working.

Stepping up beside my daughter, I took her arm, eyeing the cage where her Atlantic puffin—who was, of course, part of the ceremony—was hanging out.

"You good?"

"So good." She didn't look at me.

I figured that neither Avery nor Chris would have doubts, but it was still a relief to see them both so calm.

"Well, if I were you, I'd be nervous about the damn bird," I joked. At this point, I was desperate to lighten things up.

"Ha ha." She rolled her eyes, but she was wearing a small smile. "Puff has been practicing. We went over it multiple times yesterday."

"He's totally ready," Jana agreed.

"I can't believe we're letting a bird fly the rings down the aisle." I shook my head.

"Don't worry, Wren's got it." Jana took the puffin out of the cage and handed his lead over to Wren. "Right?"

Wren nodded, but her focus was only on the black-and-white clownlike bird. "Hey, little man. You ready to steal the show?" Her voice was soft, like she was trying not to be heard.

The wedding coordinator clapped, and Puff jumped, flapping his wings.

"Hey now. None of that." Wren resettled the bird, stroking his back softly, her tone soothing even my nerves.

I angled down to whisper to Avery as Gianna started down the aisle. "Do you know how lucky you are to have a friend willing to deal with that damn bird on your wedding day?"

Avery's throat bobbed, and she blinked twice, but she kept her focus averted. "It was her idea."

"Because she knew you and Chris would want him here."

She nodded.

"Wren's always been good to you."

She tensed next to me. Maybe that was overstepping the line she'd drawn about talking, but it was true.

Jana was halfway down the aisle before she swallowed and then turned to me. "You really like her?"

"I love her."

Avery looked down at the bouquet of red roses and white lilies in her hand. It might not have been what she wanted to hear, but it was the truth. I wasn't trying to push the idea on her, but she asked, and I wouldn't lie.

"I know you're mad at us. And I'm sorry you found out before we could tell you. I really wanted to be the one to explain. But I love her."

Avery didn't answer. As much as I wanted to push her, now wasn't the time.

Her eyes stayed locked on Wren as she walked to the door, unclipped Puff from his lead, and set him on the ground. She spoke softly to him, and then Puff took off in a half jump, half flight down the aisle.

Aws and giggles filled the air as the puffin made his way to Chris, with two rings tied around his neck.

Once he'd landed on Chris's arm, he nuzzled against his head.

"I told you he'd do it," Avery beamed, but she still hadn't looked at me. It was my fault. I'd made the day uncomfortable for her, and I felt awful about that. So I tried to force the smile.

"And now it's your turn. Ready to get married, Avy?"

Wren
33

BY THE TIME I made it down the aisle, Chris had passed Puff off to his father and the bird had been clipped to his lead.

The way both Emerson and Mr. Damiano sagged in relief once the bird was secured was almost comical.

Although none of us were willing to burst Avery's bubble and tell her that having Puff deliver the rings might be a disaster, I could almost guarantee every person here saw several scenarios involving feathers and poop that the bride didn't want to acknowledge.

With a deep breath in, I took my place with the rest of the small wedding party.

Not counting Puff, there were only six of us. Chris with his dad and Emerson, then Gianna, Jana, and me.

The music changed and I turned away from Puff. Normally I was one of those people who watched the groom as the bride came down the aisle. Today, though, my eyes were locked on Tom. And his were on me. With every step he took down the red carpet, his gaze burned into me. In this moment, I could envision a similar scene, only with the roles reversed. I could see myself walking to where he waited at the altar. Maybe for the first time ever, I didn't hate the idea of my wedding.

The thought sent butterflies fluttering in my stomach.

Like he could read my mind, he mouthed, "Someday."

When they stopped, he handed my best friend off to the man waiting for her. After the vows, the exchanging of rings, and a kiss, Avery was officially married.

When the music started, Jana stepped in front of me.

"Switch with me. You should be walking back with Tom." With a smirk, she linked arms with Chris's father and followed the bride and groom.

Gianna and Emerson were next. Then I took the three stairs down and was greeted by Tom.

With one side of his mouth lifted, he held out an arm. I eagerly accepted, and together we walked up the aisle and met up with the rest of the bridal party in the large hallway.

"Someday, baby girl." He whispered, pressing his lips to my forehead. "And I swear everyone will be happy for us."

The conviction in his voice made me want to believe it was possible.

Until my father's voice cut over the noise, and my stomach twisted.

"Wren."

Tom lifted his chin, peering over my head. "I can skip the receiving line if you want me to."

He couldn't, not really.

"I'll be fine."

I couldn't avoid my parents forever, and I had anticipated seeing them today.

With one more kiss, Tom stepped away.

Garnering all the strength I still had after this long, painful day, I turned. "Dad."

Always the picture of perfection, my dad's black suit and silver tie matched my mother's dress.

"Mom."

"You look very pretty." My mother wrung her hands, her gaze bouncing between me and my father. "Doesn't she, Heath?"

He frowned at her, then turned that expression on me. "You're not returning my calls."

"I'm not." I wanted to cross my arms, but I was still holding the damn bouquet. "We don't have much to say to one another, so what's the point?"

His nostrils flared. "You cannot date someone my age."

"He's ten years younger than you."

My father opened his mouth, but my mother stepped in front of him before he could retort.

"Wren, we just want you to be happy."

"Then take the time to learn what makes me happy."

They'd always had ideas about what my future should look like, and I'd fought them every step of the way. Today was no different.

I shook my head at the thought. Actually, it was different. "You know the wildest part of this entire thing? Tom is exactly what you've always wanted for me." I looked pointedly at my dad. "You wanted a son-in-law who would enjoy hanging out here with you." I held out one arm, gesturing to the country club. "Who would attend all the fundraisers you do. Who'd happily play a round of golf. Dad," I said, hoping like hell he'd truly hear me. "You and Tom already do that. It doesn't have to change. Mom," I said, shifting my focus. "You want a house full of family for the holidays. Well, guess what? With the Wilsons, you get that. You get me, Tom, Avery, Chris, and Chris's family. Plus a slew of kids they'll probably have. You get a family you already love."

I sighed.

"You're both so busy trying to tell me what I want that you can't see that it's been right in front of me the entire time."

My mother blinked and my father frowned. Before either could respond, I turned and walked away. The idea that the people we cared about would be happy for us was a nice one, but it didn't look like that was in the cards for us, and we'd just have to be okay with it.

Daddy Wilson
34

THE RECEPTION WAS in full swing and nothing had improved. Just a toast and the father daughter dance, and then my part of the day would be over.

With my drink in hand, I stepped up to the mic and tapped my glass. The crowd quieted. Though the massive floral arrangements made it hard to see many of the guests, there were only two people I was worried about. I turned to the bride and groom, hoping I could at least get this part of the day right.

"I doubt any of you are interested in sitting through a long speech, but since my daughter is the bride and I paid for dinner, you get to listen."

The room filled with laughter, though the guests quieted again quickly.

"Love is a funny thing, isn't it? For a long time, I had a lot of ideas about what the man who would one day marry my daughter should be." I cleared my throat, and then tossed out the thing everyone always knew about me.

"My most important stipulation was that the guy couldn't be a baseball player. See how well that worked out for me?" I pointed at

Chris.

He chuckled, along with the rest of the room.

"But that's the thing about love: you can't control it. And when two people find it—find the type of love that makes them better because of the person beside them—they have to hold on to it." My eyes scanned the room and landed on Wren. Her lips lifted in a small, encouraging smile and my chest warmed. I didn't mean this to be about us. But as I glanced over her shoulder to her father at the table behind her, I realized it did ring true for us too. "Maybe I wouldn't have picked Chris for my Avy, but over the last year, I've witnessed moment after moment that has shown me just how much he cherishes her. I've seen the way he puts her first, how he takes care of her. Respects her and adds to her life. So although he might not be who I would have picked for Avery originally, he is exactly what I always hoped she'd find. And that I can drink to." I raised my glass. "To Chris and Avery."

"To Chris and Avery," the crowd echoed.

I took a sip. Then moved to shake Chris's hand.

"Thanks." Avery nibbled on her bottom lip and didn't quite meet my eye.

"Love you, Avy." I bent down and her hair brushed my cheek as I gave her a quick kiss.

When I turned to move back to my seat as Emerson moved to the mic, I found Heath's gaze locked on me. I tipped my chin and walked right past him out the door. If he started yelling at me during Emerson's speech, my daughter would never forgive me. So if he wanted to finally talk, he'd have to follow me.

It took less than a minute before the door banged open again. "Dammit, Wilson."

I smirked. Heath actually sounded like himself. But I tempered my expression before I turned to face him.

He glared at me, his brows pulled low. "I should have known you'd find a way to say your piece even when I wouldn't talk to you."

I held both palms up as I shrugged. "It wasn't on purpose. But I promised her I'd fix this. So I am going to move heaven and earth to make you believe I'm good for your daughter."

He lowered his head and gave it a shake. "I've always believed you were a good man."

Hope ignited in my chest. I wasn't sure where he was going with this, but it could be promising.

"I didn't mean to fall in love with your daughter, but I won't apologize for it."

He ground his teeth. "Of all the women in the world."

"It's not my fault you raised the best one."

He tried, but he couldn't fight the chuckle that escaped him. "She's a pain in the ass."

"Absolutely." Heart hammering—because, shit, was he really coming to terms with this?—I slipped my hands into my pockets, willing myself to remain calm.

He shook his head at me. "And she has expensive taste."

"I'm well aware."

Finally, a ghost of a smile moved across his face. "Maybe it's good that it's you. Not many people could afford her."

It seemed to me she'd paid for her lifestyle just fine. But I wouldn't correct him, not when we were finally getting somewhere.

"If you hurt her, I'll kill you."

"I told Chris the same thing." Now that I was sure where this was heading, my shoulders relaxed.

Behind him, the door creaked open, and Wren slipped out. "My toast sucked compared to yours."

"I'm sure it was perfect, baby girl." I held out an arm in silent invitation, and without hesitation, she slipped under it and rested her hand on my hip.

To his credit, Heath didn't look away. And that felt like our first real win.

"My brain was a mess. I'm not sure the toast even made sense. I was too worried that you two were about to cause another scene." Looking from me to her dad, she gave my hip a squeeze.

"We're not." Heath pursed his lips.

Beside me, Wren sagged in defeat.

"I was just giving Tom my blessing."

She jolted under my arm, a gasp slipping from her lips. "What?"

Heath rocked back on his heels. "Hell, everything you said earlier was right." His eyes drifted shut and he shook his head. "Tom too. I don't love that you fell for my friend. I'd rather you found a man closer to your age. Someone I wasn't quite so familiar with." He opened his eyes and met mine. "But you're right. I do know Tom. I know he puts his all into the things, and the people, he loves. And you're lucky to fall into that category."

The fist around my heart loosened at his words.

As the tension drained from Wren, she stepped away and hugged her father. "Thank you."

He nodded. "But my warning stands." He lifted his chin, focus fixed on me. "Hurt her, and I'll bury you on hole six."

"Duly noted."

He roughed a hand over his face. "I never thought either of you would settle down. So maybe this makes more sense than I realized. Maybe you'll find yourself with a home in our neighborhood again one of these days." Releasing Wren, he stepped back.

Chuckling, Wren tucked herself back into my left side. "I doubt that, but he did get a new puppy."

Heath cocked a brow. "You got a dog?"

I shrugged.

"Caffrey is the cutest chocolate lab ever." She beamed up at me.

"Figures." He cleared his throat. "Like I said: expensive. You'll be redoing all those perfect hardwood floors soon."

Shit. The man wouldn't speak to me thirty minutes ago, and now he was ribbing me. This shift in the dynamic was more than I could have asked for.

"No way. Caffrey is a good boy."

I didn't know about that. The dog was still a pain in the ass, but he made Wren happy, so he was worth it.

Heath held his hand out to me. "We good?"

I kept Wren close as I accepted. "Always."

The door opened again, and this time, a blond head peeked out. "Dad?" Avery called. "It's time for our dance."

This dance was a moment I'd dreaded for months. It was going to be a last dance with my girl. But it didn't feel like the weight of the world was pressing on me for this moment anymore. It felt like the end of an era with Avery and me, but the start of a new one for both of us. One where we both had a chance at happiness. I loved my daughter, but she wasn't just my little girl anymore, and I had a life outside of being her father. It was a change for both of us, but I hoped we could move through it together.

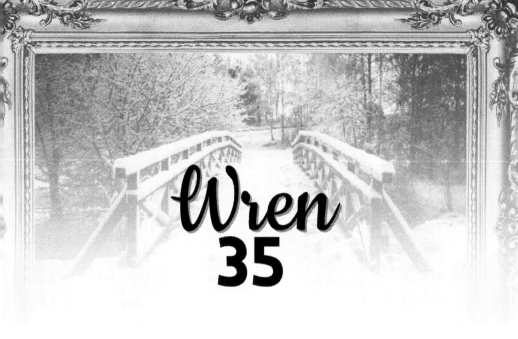

Wren
35

LIKE A HAWK, Avery tracked her father's movements until he released me and followed her inside.

"You were right to call me out for acting like a jerk." My father watched me, his hands in his pockets.

I crossed my arms over my chest.

"The last thing I want is for you to feel like the things we do for you are motivated by a need to control you."

I cocked a brow.

His shoulders slumped and his head fell. "That night at the bridal shower was not my best moment. I'm sorry about that. But I know Tom too well."

"Or not well enough," I countered. "The way he understands me. The way he makes me feel—"

"I get it." He waved me off. "I don't want the details. Please. But the rigid man I know, the one who lives the most ordered life, bought a dog for you. I get it."

I chuckled. Caffrey had added some chaos to Tom's life, sure. But he also made the man laugh. Tom might complain about every lick to his face, but his body relaxed when he snuggled with the puppy.

"I think Tom needed a little chaos in his life."

"Then you're perfect for him," my dad joked. "Come on, let's go in."

We slipped inside and headed to our seats. I moved around the outside of the mass of family and friends who had gathered around the dance floor as a Steven Curtis Chapman song played.

Of course Tom and Avery were dancing to "Cinderella." There wasn't a better song for this moment. Six months ago, Avery had jokingly asked Tom to practice dancing with her, and she'd picked this song. Being the grump he was, most would assume he'd refuse. But most would be wrong. Tom was the kind of dad who'd do anything for his child, including dance in the middle of his living room. Even my unemotional self had teared up at the sight.

I dropped into my chair at the head table and watched them as they shifted away from the crowd and moved closer. Avery's eyes met mine for one second, but she looked away quickly, like she'd done all day. Like she couldn't stand to look at me.

Where they were dancing now, I could see Tom. He was focused on his daughter, but I could see his lips and could just make out what he was saying.

"Avy, for almost thirty years, it's been you and me. I'm so proud of the woman you are. I wouldn't change a single moment."

Avery tipped her head, but I couldn't hear her response.

"I'm happy you found Chris. The guy's everything you deserve. And this moment is so much easier knowing that you're in the right place. That you found your person."

He swallowed and then blinked. And she shook her head.

"Change is inevitable. And I want us to change together. Grow into a relationship between two adults, instead of a kid and her dad." He paused for two beats before he went on. "I never want to hurt you. I just want a chance at being happy too."

They spun away, and I couldn't hear more.

I couldn't stay. I pushed to my feet and left the room. It hurt, knowing that all our relationships had changed. It wasn't supposed to be like this. My being with Tom wasn't supposed to mess up his relationship with his daughter, and it wasn't supposed to cost me my best friend.

In twenty seconds, I was out the door and in the lobby. But it wasn't enough. I needed air. As I pushed out into the cold night air, the chill bit at my bare skin.

With my arms wrapped around myself, I rubbed my arms, wishing I could slip into Tom's jacket but unwilling to go back in for it. Around me, flurries fell gently. Tom was sure Avery would get over it, but I might need to come to terms with the idea that she wouldn't. That I'd have to go on with the rest of my life without my best friend.

I swallowed down that idea, the burn of it scorching my throat.

"You must really be miserable in there if you're willing to hang out in the cold."

I gasped at the sound of my best friend's voice. "Avery." I blinked. "You shouldn't be out here."

Her eyes were shiny with tears as she stepped up next to me and wrapped an arm around my waist. Always shorter than me, her head barely came up to my shoulder.

"I do need to be out here. I have to apologize to my best friend."

"You don't—"

"I've been awful."

A long sigh escaped me, and I slumped against her. "No, I should have talked to you. I'm the one who's sorry."

She tipped her head back and made eye contact. "I didn't give you a chance to talk. My mother has pointed out that you and dad are two of my favorite people. And Jana reminded me a dozen times that we've both wanted you to find a man."

"It wasn't in my ten-year plan," I reminded her.

"Probably because I refused to let you even think about my dad that way."

She was wrong about that. I'd thought about him plenty.

Her body stiffened and her blue eyes blazed. "Please don't correct me. Those fun conversations are now between you and Jana."

She took a deep breath. "You love my dad."

My eyes flitted shut as I nodded. "I can't apologize for that."

"You don't have to."

My eyes popped open and my heart skipped.

"Something Dad said shook me." Her arm tightened around my

waist. "When I was a kid, he put all his focus into baseball and making sure I was happy. On making sure I was good. And now I'm moving on and happy. So now he should get that chance too." She took a breath. "I want that for him. And you." She cleared her throat. "So I'm sorry I was a bitch. I'm sorry I tried to write off something that was important to you. And I'm sorry I didn't listen. I wish—" Her voice cracked. She blinked and cleared her throat. "I wish I could go back to last week and try again. But neither of you have ever been relationship people." She swallowed. "The idea of a fling between you two wrecking things, leaving me to pick sides, scared me. And I reacted badly."

From that perspective, I understood where she was coming from. "We wanted to sit down and talk. Give you a chance to see us together."

"I've seen it all day." She squeezed me again. "I'm sorry I didn't see it sooner."

"I forgive you."

"Can we go inside? There is something I'd really like you to take care of for me."

I nodded and held the door open for her. "I'll do anything. What do you need?"

A small smile graced her lips as she brushed past me. "Not something to do, it's something to take care of."

Confused by her statement, all I could do was follow her. Inside, two tall, broad men in matching tuxes waited on us. Chris's eyes found Avery's instantly, but Tom stood with his arms crossed, his focus intent on the two of us.

"I'm not going to be around as much, so I could really use someone to take care of Dad." She smiled at me, blinking back the moisture in her eyes. "And I can't think of anyone better to do it."

Eyes misting over, I swallowed past the lump in my throat. "Thank you."

She threw her arms around me. "I always thought of you as family, a sister. I'll have to adjust to stepmom, I guess."

With a watery laugh, I pulled back and wiped at my eyes.

Chris cleared his throat. "Let's give these two a minute. Come dance with me, wifey."

"I love the sound of that." She gave her father a quick kiss on the cheek, then let her husband drag her back to their party.

"So." I stepped toward Tom.

"I take it she gave you her blessing?" His lips pulled up in the corners.

"You did it." I stepped closer, and when he snaked an arm around my waist and pulled me in, I went willingly. "You got everyone on board."

"I will move any mountain that stands in the way of your happiness, Wren. You can always count on that." He pulled back and grasped my hands. "Now let's go dance."

I scoffed. "I thought you didn't dance, Daddy Wilson."

"There is not much I wouldn't do for you baby girl. Plus, it's time for the entire world to find out that you're mine."

Everyone finding out that I was his? Nothing sounded better than that.

Epilogue

Daddy Wilson

I SQUATTED IN THE GRASS, leaning on the metal bat in front of me and frowning at my right fielder.

"Don't pull up, Bosco. You got to keep the swing even," I shouted.

"His bicep is probably burning." Our catcher, Asher Price, glared.

True, because the dumbass had decided to get a tattoo on his throwing arm yesterday. Not only was Bosco's fielding sucking because of it, but his swing was fucked too.

These days I might understand loving someone enough to do dumbass things, but we had games to win.

"I just hope he doesn't regret it," Asher mumbled.

"He might regret not making the big gesture more." I glanced up at the frustrated man towering over me.

I'd heard the rumors. Not from my guys, though. I actually didn't think most of the team knew. But Asher's wife had left him right before spring training.

"Wren," he muttered like a curse.

I cocked a brow. "Don't hate on the fact that our women are close. We're gone a lot. They need each other."

"You and Wren are new. Talk to me in ten years when the honeymoon is over." He shook his head.

I pushed up to my feet and leaned on the metal bat. "The relationships that last are the ones where, regardless of the day-to-day shit, the people involved don't let the honeymoon end." That was my plan with Wren.

He grunted. "I'd get ten tattoos if I thought it would help."

That was what I thought. My catcher loved his wife, and he wasn't enjoying his newfound freedom.

The question was, what was he going to do about it? Because if this miserable shit continued, it was going to be a long season.

"Maybe," I suggested, "figure out what *would* help and do that."

He glared at the field as Bosco cracked off another ball foul. "If he can't hit or throw, we're fucked."

"Bosco, watch the swing." When I turned back to Asher, he was stomping down into the dugout.

"Go easy on him, Coach." The voice ripped through me like lightning.

I shot to my feet and spun. My girl was striding my way, her red sundress blowing in the warm Florida air.

As soon as Caffrey saw me, he yanked on the black leash, pulling Wren along with him. In the two months since we'd gotten him, he'd grown enough that his paws were only slightly too big for his body.

"Easy, boy. Don't hurt Mom." I dropped the bat and chewed up the distance between us.

Caffrey jumped on my leg as I wrapped my free arm around Wren and dropped my lips to hers.

"Looking good in the pinstripes, Daddy Wilson," she mumbled against my mouth.

My heart hammered against my sternum. It had been a long three weeks without her.

She reached up and flipped my baseball cap around backward. "Loving the scruff."

"Thanks, baby girl." I kissed the inside of her wrist as she rubbed my jaw. "Not that I'm complaining, but weren't you coming tomorrow?"

I'd had the day marked in my brain since I slipped out of bed and left her three weeks ago to fly down for spring training. It had been a hell of a thing, getting her to move in formally before I left. It was a leap of faith in us, but she'd made it. It made me insanely happy, especially because I wouldn't have the time to move her in later. Once the team returned from Florida, the season would be in full swing, and I wanted the time I was home to be with her. I wanted her in my bed every night whether I was there or not. Plus, Caffrey needed her.

Normally the weeks in Florida passed quickly. I didn't know whether it was because some of my guys were extra moody or because I was missing Wren, but time had crept slowly while we'd been apart.

"We missed you, so we hopped on an earlier flight."

"Best surprise ever."

Caffrey jumped up again and licked at my uniform.

Begrudgingly, I let go of Wren to give the puppy some attention. She handed me his leash as I got down on my knee. He flopped onto his back, and I rubbed his belly.

"How the hell did you get the dog down on the field?" I glanced up at her, shielding my eyes from the sun with one hand.

"Like this." She donned a flirty smile that made my heart skip and flipped her sunglasses up. "Please can't I bring him down to see his daddy?" She batted her eyes and pushed her lip out in a pout.

Hauling myself upright again, I hooked an arm around her neck and yanked her into me. "Don't flirt with my security guards, baby girl."

She giggled. "Don't worry. I love you best."

"Damn right, you do."

"Wren." Avery's shriek ripped through the air. "Come here!"

My girl ducked out of my arms heading toward her best friend. I wanted to be annoyed, but the sight of Avery leaning over the fence to hug her while they laughed made my heart squeeze. For too long, I wasn't sure those two would get back to the friendship they once had.

But they were closer than ever. So close, in fact, that they'd tried to convince Chris and me that the four of us should stay together while the girls were in town.

Luckily my son-in-law was on the same page as me, and we rented houses next door to each other instead. The girls could slip through the fence and have coffee in the morning, but Chris and I each had our own space. I loved my daughter, but I refused to share a wall with her.

Avery passed a white bundle over the wall to Wren, and my eyes narrowed. What were they up to now?

Dramatically, Wren shook out the shirt. At the sight of it, my breath caught. Avery had been wearing my throwback jersey for years, but when Wren slipped her arms into the sleeves and spun, I swore my heart stopped. My name emblazoned on her back was something else.

"You look damn good in number forty-nine, baby girl," I called over.

She batted her eyes. "Seems like it's my number." Slowly, she moved back toward me. "Almost like it was meant to be."

I couldn't help but smile. Although we hadn't gotten here quickly or easily, I'd never been happier. I'd always sought out calm control, but all this time, I'd really just needed a touch of chaos. And finding out exactly what I needed was the best thing to ever happen to me.

Want to see what happens with Asher and if he can fix his marriage and win Zara back?
The Freak Out Coming 2025

DEAR READER

First, let me just say a massive THANK YOU for reading Finding Out.

This book was such a happy accident. When I started The Fall Out, I never planned for Coach Wilson to have a book, but the second Wren and Daddy Wilson appeared on page together, it became clear their story needed to be written. And what a fun dramatic not quite novella it became.

I've loved the Revs series so far, and I can't believe in one book these boys will be finished! Who is ready for Asher and Zara? I know I am.

If you haven't yet, definitely jump back to the Momcoms for Beckett and Liv's and Cortney and Dylan's stories. Then check out Mason and his trainer's story in Gracie York's (My pen name with AJ Ranney) Back Together Again.

Finally, remember: Live in your world, fall in love in mine.

Jenni

ACKNOWLEDGMENTS

A big thank you to my kids. You all are my favorite people, and put up with a lot of baseball and book talk. Thank you for giving me the time and support to get these books done.

Thank you to my parents, who support me in everything I do all the time. I couldn't get through life without you guys. Being able to count on you both for help, support, or encouragement is the best gift. Thank you for the many many hours and days of babysitting so I can go to events and signings. I couldn't do this without you! Thank you for being examples I can strive to be with my kids and being the best grandparents ever.

Beth, thank you for being you. Detailed, and organized because I am not. And your series bibles are amazing. You are a friend and such an amazing supporter of me. I will never stop singing your praises from the rooftops. You rock at your job, and we all know it! Thank you for being the wonderful person you are.

Becca and the rest of the Author agency you all are the best. You keep up with me and always have things under control. I'm chaos and I'm sure I make you nuts with the 'wait, when is the cover reveal' messages, I constantly send your way.

Sara, thank you for everything. There aren't enough words to explain what you are. A friend, a support, a cheerleader, and an amazing visually creative gem, I'm so lucky to have you. You wear so many hats, not just for me but for all the authors you work with. You do it all and juggle so many things it makes my head spin. But whenever I need one more thing you get it done. I'm so proud of the amazing business you created and I can't wait to watch you keep flying.

Jeff, thank you for being the final nit-picky check to make sure everything is perfect. Becoming a romance reader wasn't on your to do list, but I'm grateful you did it anyway!

Britt, thank you for being you. I probably could do things without you, but I wouldn't want to. I can't believe I was lucky enough that you recognized a random beach one February day. Your support is never ending, even when you are so busy with your own stuff. Watching you soar in your success is inspiring. I love getting to be part of every new idea you have. You are the best.

Jess, thank you for always being my cheerleader, and listening to my next idea. I'm so grateful to not only get to work with you, but also to call you a friend.

Shani, I can't thank you enough for all your support and expert sticker making. You never stop singing the Revs' praises and I'm so blessed to have you on my teams. You are creative and amazing!

Amy, thank you for being the organized one, the one that keeps us on track, and the one that makes sure we get it done. For putting up with my chaos and my next 'fun' thing. I'm so lucky to get to call you one of my best friends. Daphne, thank you for being an amazing friend and always helping. Anna, thank you for being a great friend and helping whenever I need a beta reader. Andi, thank you for always being willing to add one more job, I'm so glad to have you on our team. Charity I'm so glad you joined our team and want to be on this crazy adventure with us! I'm grateful for your support and friendship. Kenzie and Courtney you two both own TikTok and I am so glad to have your help with that!

Rick, all the rest of Hambright, thank you for taking a chance on me and helping to make this release awesome.

And a big thank you to the rest of my friends and family who have helped me with encouragement and feedback. I love you all and am so thankful for your support.

ABOUT THE AUTHOR

Jenni Bara lives in New Jersey, working as a paralegal in family law, writing real-life unhappily ever-afters every day. In turn, she spends her free time with anything that keeps her laughing, including life with four kids. She is just starting her career as a romance author writing books with an outstanding balance of life, love, and laughter.

ALSO BY JENNI BARA

Want more Boston Revs Baseball

Mother Maker - Cortney Miller

The Fall Out - Christian Damiano

Back Together Again - Mason Dumpty

The Fake Out - Emerson Knight

The Foul Out - Kyle Bosco

Finding Out - Coach Wilson

The Freak Out - Asher Price

More By Jenni Bara

Curious about the baseball boys from the NY Metros

NY Metros Baseball

More than the Game

More than a Story

Wishing for More

c2c0859d-aa20-4f6c-922d-0086aee51ab6R02